Hawley Smart

Sunshine and Snow

Vol. 2

Hawley Smart

Sunshine and Snow
Vol. 2

ISBN/EAN: 9783337258306

Printed in Europe, USA, Canada, Australia, Japan

Cover: Foto ©Andreas Hilbeck / pixelio.de

More available books at **www.hansebooks.com**

SUNSHINE AND SNOW

A Novel.

BY

HAWLEY SMART,

AUTHOR OF "BREEZIE LANGTON," "TWO KISSES," "BROKEN BONDS,"
"BOUND TO WIN," ETC. ETC.

IN THREE VOLUMES.

VOL. II.

London :

CHAPMAN AND HALL, 193, PICCADILLY.

1878.

CONTENTS.

CHAPTER XI.

CHAPTER XII.

CHAPTER XIII.

CHAPTER XIV.

SUNSHINE AND SNOW.

CHAPTER I.

APPOINTED TO THE STAFF.

GONE—not a line, not a message ; and he had been deluding himself with the idea that this girl cared about him. He had been but the victim of a practised gambler, the dupe of a clever coquette. He had paid, he had declined to play further. Why waste time over the goose who had been plucked to the extent that he could be brought to submit to ? why waste smiles upon a love-lorn swain, who had suddenly become blind to the fascinations of écarté ? Could anything be clearer than that Lydon, seeing the attraction Clarisse was, had craftily used his daughter as a lure, and, plundering his prey to the outside of his ability, had then, folding his tents like the Ismaelite he was, moved silently away.

Yes, what an unmitigated fool he had been. It was not the money, no, d—n that; but it was with a ghastly grimace Jim Hawksbury owned to himself that Clarisse Lydon had taken much more than that from him. He had thought her so true, so honest, so genuine; he had believed in her, despite appearances; he had believed in her father for her sake; he had loved her, and now—had he been a wooer to jeer at? had it been a jest to see him stripped nightly of his substance by her astute father? · He didn't know. He ground his teeth as men are wont when they first discover that if woman is won-drous fair, she at times can be wondrous false. Clarisse had stolen from him that best part of man's nature—belief in her own sex. If that bright, frank face could woo him to undoing, and leave him without a word when she deemed that her influence for his undoing was no longer necessary, how place faith in woman in future? And yet it seemed so hard to believe that she had not been in earnest about her regrets at his losses, that her remonstrance against his high play with her father should be all a sham. Still, what did this flitting without a word mean? Did it not look as if Mr. Lydon, having got his money, would fain escape questioning or chance of recognition, should the victim chance to bemoan the loss of his skin in public places? and Jim had heard wailings in smoking-rooms over similar chastisement give rise to sharp comment or fierce invective against "the brave who had raised hair" on such occasions.

It is some consolation in our foolishness to know, that it is confined to ourselves and not babbled among our acquaintance.

This slight solace, so far as it went, Jim

was in possession of, for except Cherriton,
no one of his friends knew anything of
the intimacy with the Lydons, and even
the Chirper knew but little concerning it ;
that the écarté inaugurated that wet
evening in Cleveland Row had developed
into genuine high play and considerably
to Hawksbury's detriment, Mr. Cherriton
had as yet no conception.   That Jim visited
the Lydons a good deal, and that Miss
Lydon was a pretty girl, he did know ;
but his knowledge went no farther, and
he had never even seen Clarisse.

Still, the young man in love who does
not more or less afflict some one of his
friends with his confidences is a pheno-
menon.   Jim Hawksbury was a tolerably
sensible, well-balanced-minded man of his
years. He had no far-fetched romance about
his character.   He could be fairly reticent
about his hopes and fears, his joys and
tribulations, but that he should altogether
refrain from speaking of Clarisse was hardly

to be expected. Mr. Cherriton had heard about the Lydons from Donaldson, be it remembered, in the first instance. He had met the artist himself at The Vacuna ; the Chirper was Jim's most intimate friend. What wonder, therefore, that the name of Clarisse Lydon was familiar to him, and that he knew his esteem was rather sweet in that quarter. Of the écarté Mr. Cherriton knew nothing, nor did he apprehend that Jim's intimacy with Grove Terrace was to be looked at in any other light than that of pardonable flirtation. He had never seen his brother-sub. seriously affected in this wise, and regarded him as particularly well able to take care of himself.

Jim, back at Aldershot, sits in his hut, smoking doggedly, and turning over the events of the last seven or eight weeks in his mind—mental faculties still busy with that blow to his *amour propre* to think that a girl's bright eyes should have so dulled his intelligence, that no sheep could have submitted to the shearer more placidly than he. Love and exasperation still struggling for the mastery in his soul, for that he does love this girl, be she nothing but the ground-bait of a gambler's trap, he cannot deny. He has not experienced, but he has heard of such things, especially in Paris, how the daughters of Circe, with malice prepense, have lured their adorers to the fatal tables, nor ceased their maddening witcheries till the victim, his final stake played, was himself tabled at last in the Morgue. A sharp tap at the door cuts the thread of these gloomy reflections, and a non-commissioned officer enters with his letters. He looks carelessly at them—two—and both in unknown handwriting. He wonders whether either of them is destined to explain this mysterious disappearance of the Lydons. A woman's hand this, surely, though a little quaint and precise, not quite a girl's hand either, he thinks, as he breaks the seal.

" My dear Jim,

" I am not given nowadays
to correspondence with light dragoons,
but an avaricious old woman, when she
has made an investment, never leaves a
stone unturned to prevent its turning out
profitable. Lending you money would
never have been looked upon as a good
speculation by anyone but your grandmamma or a professional money-lender, but
then you see I'm so cunning. Sir Richard
Bowood has got the Canadian command,
and has promised to take you out as his
aide. That is nice for you, and I insist
upon your taking it, or, sir, I may proceed
to extremities, and—well, I don't know
quite what, but make myself disagreeable.
Of course I am jesting about the money,
but the appointment is a good thing for
you. Sir Richard, I believe, you know a
little, and I am sure you will find him
pleasant as a chief. I knew him quite as
a boy ; I was nearly saying when I was

a young woman, but you know I'm that
now, and only gave up flirtation and
dancing a year or two ago.   Come up to
lunch next Thursday, kiss hands upon your
appointment, and let me formally present
you to your future general.   I have assured
him, Heaven forgive me, that the management of a household is your peculiar forte,
and your judgment of claret undeniable.
I think Letty and myself must really put
you through a course of instruction, as I
told Sir Richard that nobody understood
an aide-de-camp's duties more thoroughly
than I did.   Congratulations, my dear Jim,
in which Letty most cordially joins.   For
me, I always consider it bad taste on your
part to have grown up and commenced
the wearing of moustaches before I had
made up my mind to become an old woman.
However, in this generation boys won't be
boys, nor grandmothers grandmothers.

"Your affectionate grandmamma

"all the same,

"MARIANNE HAWKSBURY."

"What a trump the old lady is," muttered Jim, as he finished the epistle with a laugh on his lips. "How kind of her, and it so like her to make a jest of her goodness. I can only say I rather pity fellows who haven't grandmothers just now. Well, I wonder what this other epistle is about; however, after plunging into the first, one need not augur ill of the second."

The second, indeed, was a mere corroboration of the first, being simply an offer from Sir Richard Bowood to place him upon his staff, he having had the good fortune to receive the Canadian command, with an intimation that he would find no difficulty on the subject with the authorities should he be willing to accept, and that he, Sir Richard, did not purpose going out till the beginning of September.

"It's very odd," mused Jim; "deuce take it. I never did believe much in destiny, but I'll be hung if this don't look like it; that girl is my destiny for good or evil, and it don't like being for good as far as our acquaintance has gone. She has disappeared; of course gone to Canada, and now I am about to follow her."

A knock at the door was followed by the appearance of Mr. Cherriton, almost before Hawksbury had time to bid him enter.

"What made you cut mess, Jim, in such early fashion?" inquired the Chirper, as he threw himself into an arm-chair; "perhaps, on the whole, you were right; whether it was worth while stopping to hear Clarkson recount how he lost the regimental cup last autumn for the twenty-seventh time, and to lose three rubbers running, is open to question."

"I wanted to have a good think," replied Hawksbury, "and so came home to have a solitary cigar."

"Ah well, I suppose you've got through with it," observed the Chirper, with easy nonchalance. "I can only hope more will come of it than usually comes of mine."

"I am about to leave the regiment," returned Hawksbury, with great gravity.

"No! good heavens, why? You don't mean that!" exclaimed Cherriton, springing to his feet. "Think well what you are about, Jim! You wouldn't leave the old corps lightly, I know. What is it?"

"Well, I'm not going to leave it altogether, only in a temporary sort of way. The fact is, I am going on Sir Richard Bowood's staff to Canada."

"By Jove, what a bit of luck! I congratulate you with all my heart; though no one will be more sorry to lose you than I shall be."

"Yes, it is falling into a good thing," replied Jim, slowly. "My grandmother, old Lady Hawksbury, managed it for me. I tell you what, Chirper, a grandmother isn't a bad sort of thing to have at times. Just you sit down again, and I'll let you know what has happened to me of late."

Mr. Cherriton listened in silence, though

with avidious and undisguised astonishment,
to. Jim's narration of how that quiet écarté
commenced in Cleveland Row had culmi-
nated. When Hawksbury told how the
Dowager had come to the rescue, his eyes
sparkled with admiration, and he anathema-
tised the fortune that had bereft him of
such a charming and interesting relation.

"Look here, Jim," he exclaimed, "if
you'll take two spinster aunts' expectations
in, and fifty to boot, for your grandmother,
it's a deal."

He shook his precocious head over the
card-playing, and looked at Jim while ex-
patiating on Clarisse's charms and perfec-
tions with an air of sympathetic tolerance.
It is easy to regard your friend with slightly
contemptuous pity who admits himself to
be within the toils, when personally you
have not encountered Circe. What fools
the followers of Ulysses must have appeared
to the good people of Athens when that
little historiette got bruited abroad.

"What do you think of it all?" inquired Jim, as he concluded.

"Hum," replied Mr. Cherriton, as he puffed leisurely at his cigar. "I'm afraid there is only one explanation to be put upon it, that you have been scientifically legged. It's just possible, you know," he continued a little hastily upon seeing his host's impatient gesture, "that the young woman wasn't in it, although I confess to me it looks very much as if she was her father's confederate."

"You never saw her," retorted Jim, curtly.

"No, you're quite right, I never did; but I think perhaps I am a better judge for not having done so. It's not easy, I know, to believe such things of a pretty, lady-like girl; but such things have been, old man."

"Yes," replied Jim, as he leant his head upon his hand, "of course I'm aware of that. I suppose you're right in this case, but, confound it, I'd give all I have, or ever hope to have, not to think so."

" When are you off to Canada ?" inquired Cherriton, by way of changing the conversation.

" Not till September; but I am to go up to lunch with the old lady, and be introduced to Sir Richard on Thursday. Come too, she'll be delighted to see you, and Miss Auriole always inquires after you."

" It's a bargain, Jim," replied the Chirper, solemnly. " A grandmother like yours is a sight to travel miles to see. Some people crave to behold royalty, some monstrosities, some new countries, some new pictures or celebrities; but to my mind an elderly relation, with so delicate a sense of an elderly relation's obligations, is an object far surpassing any of these. What are material beauties compared to mental ? Do you suppose Pope would ever have described ' an honest man ' as ' the noblest

work of God' if he had ever encountered
a munificent grandmother? Here's Lady
Hawksbury the elder, God bless her!"
concluded Cherriton, as he finished his
brandy-and-water. "May she long con-
tinue her career of well-applied benevolence!
and now good-night."

So saying, Mr. Cherriton took his departure, and Hawksbury betook himself to
his bed.

Clad in shining raiment and with decorated button-holes, the young men presented
themselves in Park Lane on Thursday, a
few minutes before two. They were both
cordially welcomed by the Dowager and
Miss Auriole, and then presented to Jim's
future chief, Sir Richard Bowood. A tall,
slight, wiry man, with grizzled moustache
and slightly pompous manner; courteous
very, deferent indeed to ladies, but always
with just that slight tinge of egoism which
it is impossible to overlook; you could
never imagine Sir Richard forgetting for

one moment that he was Lieut.-General Sir
Richard Bowood, K.C.B., although at the
same time it was not offensively obtruded
upon one.

"Very glad, Mr. Hawksbury, to have
you with me," said the General. "Her
Ladyship, and indeed all your family are
old friends of mine. I hope you and I
shall be able to say the same before we
part."

"I trust so, Sir Richard," returned Jim,
quietly.

"There's a rumour," laughed the General,
" that we are to see service. The Knights
of the Golden Circle, whatever they may be,
it is reported, are likely to give trouble
and stir up rebellion, or Yankee filibustering
expeditions, or something of that kind. By
Jove, Lady Hawksbury, you'll hear of my
having a little affair of my own; a '48
Cavaignac business in Montreal."

"I trust not, Sir Richard," rejoined the
old lady; "it would make you dreadfully

unpopular; and it's quite possible, you know, I might take it into my head to pay you a visit this winter."

The Dowager spoke in jest. She was accustomed to talk of going here, there, and everywhere, in this airy and volatile fashion, and she did at times dearly like to astonish her friends by keeping her word; but she certainly, at that moment, did not contemplate wintering in the West.

" Of course," chimed in Jim, "you know you are fond of a change, grandmamma; and a look at the sleighing, the snows, and Niagara, would suit you down to the ground."

"I'm sure Lady Hawksbury may rely upon my endeavouring to make such a trip pleasant to her," observed Sir Richard, with a courtly obeisance.

" Oh dear, Letty, do you hear all this ?" cried the Dowager, laughing; " they ignore my rheumatism and all the rest of it, and are verily inclined to believe that I am as

young as I would fain make myself out
to be."

" No wonder," replied Miss Auriole;
" you compel us to take you on your
own valuation of your infirmities; and I
never hear about that rheumatism, unless
the invitation is not at all to your
liking."

" Mr. Cherriton," exclaimed the Dowager,
with mock solemnity, " have you a grandmother ? "

" No, unfortunately," responded the
Chirper, with considerable fervour, bearing
in mind what the old lady had so recently
done for his *fidus Achates*, and most devoutly wishing that he were blessed with
a relation of similarly broad and sympathetic views.

" If you had," resumed Lady Hawksbury,
merrily, " I am sure you would not wish
to imperil her precious life as these children
propose to do mine. What would be your
feelings if you found yourself amongst these

Knights of the—what is it?—ah, Golden Circle?"

"Punch their heads—no, I beg pardon," replied the Chirper, "put 'em down, and all that sort of thing."

"The same idea, Mr. Cherriton," said Miss Auriole, laughing, but not so tersely expressed.

"Awfully sorry; I didn't mean to say it; but really, you know," said the Chirper, in much confusion.

"It's what suits the democratic element best when they get overweeningly bumptious," interposed the Dowager, who was all for meeting the upheaval of the masses with a hand of iron.

An upheaval, by-the-way, steady, though gradual, and by no means to be suppressed any longer in these times; to be guided, perhaps, but not to be put down by derision or violence, as is now tolerably well acknowledged.

Mr. Cherriton's regret that he does not

possess a grandmother waxes deeper and deeper. "Let her go to Canada?" he mutters, "never! catch me allowing such endangering of her valuable life."

"But tell me, Sir Richard," exclaims Miss Auriole, "what are these Knights of the Golden Circle you allude to?"

"We don't know precisely, but believe them to be the Canadian organisation of the Irish republican party—a party that thinks an insurrectionary movement in our American colonies would furnish them similar opportunity at home. They seem to have forgotten '48 and Smith O'Brien's fiasco. If there wasn't a soldier in Ireland, and we withdrew from that island to-morrow, it's not the young Ireland or Fenian party that would dispose of her destinies, though they believe so, but the stalwart Orangemen from Ulster who would speedily obtain the upper hand."

"Mr. Cherriton," inquired Letty, in a low tone, "I don't forget our conversation at Ringstone Abbey. Have you discovered how I am to advance your interests ?"

"Not quite, but I begin to see," replied the Chirper, in confidential tones, "what I told you was truth. Here it is before you. Lady Hawksbury got Jim his appointment. His own knowledge of tobacco, horseflesh, and military matters stood him in no stead whatever."

"And you think a similar opportunity will be vouchsafed me."

"Who would doubt it, Miss Auriole?" rejoined the Chirper, gaily. "I only beg you to remember that you have promised to exercise it in my behalf."

"I shall not forget when the time comes," rejoined the young lady, laughing.

Destined to come in a way neither of the speakers dreamt of. Somewhat curious to note in the philosophy of life how the jest of the minute comes home to roost in bitter earnest at last. Laughing lips speak lightly of being ruined on the race-course, or at the

card-table, where the stakes have been
bagatelles. A few years later, and they
perchance tell the same story, with
quivering mouth, and — God help them,
poor souls!—very little laughter about the
recital.

CHAPTER II.

"THE KNIGHTS OF THE GOLDEN CIRCLE."

THE elder sisters of the British Isles have been much exercised from time immemorial by the terrible goings on of the family Cinderella. There is no counting upon what indiscretion that junior member of the family will commit. She throws herself into the arms of the Scarlet Lady of Babylon, or embraces Madame La République with similar fervour and lack of discrimination. She imagines herself afflicted with all sorts of ailments; she is given to all sorts of vapours; she flirts indiscriminately with all descriptions of filibustering foreigners; she shocks both decorous England and puritanical Scotland by her wild shrieking and trumpeting; she has had her ears boxed; she has been soothed and petted, but neither ferule nor sugar-plums have any permanent effect upon this young and malcontent sister. One thing clear, especially clear to her legal and necessitous advisers, that she must have separate maintenance.

It is true that in years gone by Cinderella was kept by her elder sisters pretty close to the ash-pit, and that in those days a very great if somewhat vituperative man, standing up for her rights, did make demand for the sinews of war necessary to organise powerful agitation. Poor Cinderella, she found the money—God knows how—but when the liberator who had done so much for her was laid to rest, there were not wanting Brummagem imitators, who not only proposed with airy audacity to fill his place, but thought nothing more grievous could happen to those taking charge of

Cinderella's affairs, than that "the Rint" should be laid to rest also. For many years the patriots of Hibernia, or "those wanting place" according to Fielding's definition, have traded upon this idea of "separate maintenance." I fancy our fair sister will be nearer the ash-pit again than she has been for some years should she ever obtain it, the domestic economics being a point never well understood by her children.

But about this time it occurred to a noble band of Irishmen that, having nothing earthly to lose and nothing in particular to do, it was time to dedicate themselves to freeing their oppressed country from the thraldom of the accursed Saxon. This may be described as a constitutional emotion, certain to recur to the unemployed Celt after his third tumbler of punch, but as a rule it does not take definite shape. Still, occasionally it will, and that ludicrous struggle amongst the cabbages in '48 yet testifies to what may come of it when, gathering like an avalanche, the frothy speeches and furious denunciations at last descend in practical form upon our bewildered heads. These patriotic Irishmen of the last decade were neither men of much intelligence nor much breadth of view. That "England's weakness was Ireland's opportunity" they trumpeted forth far and wide, and that England must be embroiled with the United States shortly they advertised as a fact patent to all mankind. Revolution in Ireland and the invasion of Canada from America, that was their programme. Funds were urgently required for the great Fenian movement, and the organisation of the Knights of the Golden Circle in Canada. One thing quite certain to the promoters of the new movement, that "the Rint" was likely to come in again under a new form, and whether it was "Ireland's opportunity" or no, it was undoubtedly theirs—much money to be made in contracting for pikes, muskets, boots, &c. ; moreover, you cannot be called to very strict account concerning subscriptions received for an illegal purpose.

The old showman-business of blare of trumpet and strident vociferation will deceive mankind till the end of time, and the Government were not more unreasonably imposed upon than it was natural to suppose. They did know that this organisation not only existed, but to very considerable extent in Ireland; equally were they aware of how weak in interest and inconsequent it was. Still, they deemed it of a strength that might occasion much mischief, and perhaps loss of life, in any district where it might happen to take tumouric shape, come to a head, and burst —tumour to be speedily cured by sharp exercise of the knife, of course ; but our rulers of to-day are far wiser than those of bygone times, and infinitely prefer anodyne treatment to surgery. But, about how this strange society was getting on in

Canada and America, Government were
not quite so well informed, and they were
advised from there that with so many disbanded soldiers as were at present lounging
about New York, Vermont, and Massa-
chusetts, in consequence of the termination
of the great struggle between North and
South, it was quite likely that filibustering expeditions on a large scale might be
attempted across the Canadian frontier.

Lieut.-General Bloomingdale, at that time
commanding in the Canadas, was one of
that type with which the British army has
never been without, and of which moreover
it is sincerely to be hoped it never will be.
A bluff, wiry old trooper, who had seen
much hard service in the Crimea. Indeed,
a man who in American parlance was always
" spoiling for a fight," and felt exceedingly
jealous if blows were come to in any part
of the vast English empire without his
being there to assist in their administering.
Not a scientific warrior, his decriers con-

tended, rather too ready to put affairs to the stern arbitrament of battle without due reckoning of the probabilities in his favour, but withal dogged and tenacious; extremely slow to believe that he was getting the worst of things. Just the man from one point of view to deal with a filibustering expedition, as being likely to handle them with a terrible roughness and disregard of life, which produces much panic in such half-disciplined raiders at the outset, and usually leads to their total evaporation. On the other hand, hardly diplomatic enough for such delicate relations as the Government thought fit to consider subsisted between ourselves and the United States. General Bloomingdale had one steady, fixed idea, that poachers on his estate, *i.e.* the estate of which he was keeper, caught with guns in their hands, were to be put down promptly and roughly, without appeal to consuls, ambassadors, or anyone else. That a short shrift, the nearest tree, with a slight

preliminary, perhaps, of a drum-head court-
martial, was the best remedy for those who
led the rabble arcoss their neighbours' lands
for purposes of revolution and plunder. A
dangerous man this, thought the English
Government, at such a delicate crisis. The
bluff, fiery old soldier had done too good
service to be superseded, but the expiration
of his time of command they hailed with
signal satisfaction ; they felt that, very
unlike Sir Richard Strachan,

> Impatient to be at 'em,
> He *wouldn't wait* for the Earl of Chatham.

The veteran of course applied to be left in
command for another year or so under the
circumstances. When throats were to be
cut, or killing to be done, had he ever failed
to pray to be allowed a share in it ? but the
Secretary for War took refuge, of course,
in that mythical shadow the " rule of the
service," and regretted that he must relieve
him.

The tough old General, however, did his best as long as it depended upon him. He had seen too much of the slackness with which Government usually treats the requests of an officer for reinforcements who has to meet a colonial difficulty, not to know the importance of applying for them in good time. He represented to the authorities that the extent of the Canadian frontier was very large; that this Fenian filibustering raid was a thing extremely probable; that it would be most speedily and thoroughly extinguished, if ever it should take place, he could pledge his word; but in the meantime he wanted more troops, most especially a cavalry regiment. " Nothing permanent could come of it," concluded the General, " as the sympathisers with the movement in this country are few and far between; but much local misery and destruction of property might be occasioned from inefficient guarding of the salient points of our boundary offering attack. Aided admirably as I am by

the Canadians themselves, I have still hardly
troops enough to prevent this, although I
can thoroughly answer for any filibustering
expedition obtaining no hold upon the country
unless backed openly by the United States
Government."

The Ministry for once were wide awake
to the fact that prevention in this case was
wise and economical, an idea which, did it
occur to them more constantly, would prevent
a goodly number of those small wars into
which we so continually drift. That the
presence of a regiment would prevent the
encroachment which a mere corporal's guard
provokes is, upon the whole, worthy of consideration. The maintenance of a sufficient
military force for fifty years will cost less
than a twelvemonth's warfare ; but then we
really must consider the budget, and what
we want is cheap government—not much
matter about good, but especially let it be
cheap. What signifies strength, endurance,
welding, consolidation of the empire, &c. ?

Bah ! Give us a State-coach strong enough to hold together for our day, and we ask no more, for this is the era of shoddyhood, and shoddy, sitting in high places, gives gorgeous banquets, droppeth its h's into its turtle, and prescribes to us that we should live for ourselves and the present. Shoddy, of Stock Exchange and financial scheming generally, may be right, for it is devoutly to be hoped for them that there is no hereafter.

Sir Richard Bowood was a general of great though mysterious interest. Possessed of most courtly manners and perfect tact, he had always been popular in his several commands, more especially with the civil element under his rule. With good private means, he invariably entertained liberally, and had a singular knack of ingratiating himself with the leading people in his vicinity. The soldiers liked him, for, though a smart officer, he was not given to harassing them unnecessarily. Then he was always willing to promote sport or gaiety of any kind—

theatricals, balls, a day's steeple-chasing, or a day's cricketing. Sir Richard was ever free with both his patronage and purse for their promotion. Decidedly the man for the Canada command, said the Ministry, and assuredly it would have been easier to make infinitely worse selection. The sole objection that could be urged with any justice against Sir Richard was, that he had been singularly unlucky throughout his career in the matter of active service. The very converse of General Bloomingdale, it had always been his ill fate to be employed somewhere else when hostilities broke out. A sore point rather with Sir Richard to this day that he should never have taken part in a campaign. His K.C.B. even had been gained for diplomatic service, and not won upon the field of battle. Still, despite all this, military men believed in him, and had much faith that Bowood would be quite equal to his opportunity when he got it.

It is curious, very, this valuation of men

by their fellows. How, in his particular set, a man somehow gets credit for good qualities. It is believed that he could do pretty well anything if he chose to try. Sometimes he does ; and then, alas ! comes a shattering of the idol we have worshipped, and a discovery of the very half-baked clay which formed its pediment, mixed with astonishment that such flimsy foundation should have sustained it so long. Simultaneously that silent, unobtrusive individual, whom we rarely condescended to bid good-day, turns out to have painted the picture, or written the play, of the season.

The authorities, talking matters over with Sir Richard, of course acquaint him with the opinion of General Bloomingdale, and inform him that they propose to strengthen the command by two regiments of infantry, two batteries of artillery, and a regiment of hussars. They hint pretty broadly that they consider this will be reinforcing the Canadian army very ex-

tensively, and that, except under unforeseen
circumstances, they consider the Canadian
Commander-in-chief will have most ample
means at his disposal for dealing with any
filibustering raids that may be the outcome
of the Fenian agitation. More especially is
Sir Richard enjoined to be careful about
proceeding to extremities, and that, in
Ministerial eyes, it will be deemed more
satisfactory if, by strong demonstration,
unlicensed marauders can be frightened
back across the border, than they should be
sent back shrieking, after undergoing rough,
if well-merited, chastisement. It was the
giving of instructions to play the game of
bluff against a people, of all others, pre-
eminent at that diversion ; but a pusilla-
nimity, not particularly creditable to our
rulers, has usually characterised our dealings
with the United States—a shrewd, quick-
witted people, no whit more disposed to
quarrel with us than we with them in
reality, but too keen at a bargain not to

indulge in bluff when they think it may serve their purpose, and not without due judgment, as the Oregon question and the Alabama claims bear testimony.

When Sir Richard makes reference to his wish to take Mr. Hawksbury on his personal staff, and presumes there will be no objection, he is informed, on the contrary, he could not have made a more fortunate selection in one sense, as that identical regiment of hussars is the one Government propose despatching to Canada. Great intelligence this for Mr. Cherriton, when it shall reach him, as it naturally will, in due course; but Sir Richard has small thought of that audacious cornet just now, though destined to be reminded of his existence pretty frequently later on.

On one point the authorities were somewhat urgent, and that was, that Sir Richard should take up his appointment with no unnecessary delay.

"These reinforcements go out at once,"

said that shadowy Excellency from whom
the new Commander-in-chief of the Canadas
received his instructions; "and in the
present state of affairs, it would be most
unadvisable that you should not be there
before Bloomingdale leaves. A man in
temporary command cannot carry the same
weight with the Canadian Government as
you would do; and between ourselves, we
are a little afraid of what Bloomingdale
might do. If it was a simple question of
fighting we could trust him, but it is a much
more delicate question—namely, maintaining
the inviolability of the frontier without
bloodshed if possible."   ·

"I am no believer in the application of
blank cartridges, my lord," replied Sir
Richard, dryly. "It may frighten old
women and children, but not men."

"Pooh, don't misunderstand me. We
don't tie your hands in that way, but we
expect you not to mow down raiders with
shot and shell if it is possible to scare them

without it. Capital officer, Bloomingdale,
but rather the man to let a Fenian mob
know their mistake pretty sharply. He
bears the reputation of a hardish hitter with
us, and dealt out devilish high justice in
the Indian Mutiny."

"A case in which it was a stern necessity
if we were to hold India," retorted Sir
Richard.

"Well, perhaps so," replied his Excellency, carelessly. "Never mind, you understand what we want *now*," and he
emphasized the last word strongly. "Any
arrangements about your personal staff of
course we shall be delighted to accede to.
For the present, I have no more than to
wish you *bon voyage*, though, of course, I
shall see you again before you sail."

Sir Richard Bowood bowed and left the
room, meditating as he walked back to his
club about the pleasantness of having his
hands and judgment shackled upon what
might prove to be an emergency, requiring

stern, sharp, and uncompromising treatment. Better, perhaps, to have a truculent
reputation such as Bloomingdale's than be
esteemed the combination of soldier and
diplomatist he was.

CHAPTER III.

SIR RANDOLPH HAWKSBURY, still nursing
his wrath against his first-born, is making
the house as unpleasant as may be to his
wife and daughter. He reminded them of
the hero of the old anecdote, who "was as
disagreeable as circumstances permitted,"
and they were both fain to admit in their
different ways that they were having a hard
time of it. The baronet, now he has discovered that his wife had urged this pet
scheme of his upon Jim as unsuccessfully as
himself, persists in regarding his son's rebellion as the result of premature indiscretion on her part—insists strenuously that if

it had not been for her botching, boggling manœuvring, there would have been no difficulty at all about bringing it about, and avails himself generally of those manifold opportunities which present to the lord of the household for nagging. He enjoyed also the supreme aggravation of knowing in his own heart that he was thoroughly in the wrong. Uncle Robert had told him bluntly that he did not think he had any right to refuse to help his only son out of so small a scrape. Small pecuniarily, that is, with reference to Sir Randolph's income, and his brother was the one man for whose opinion the Baronet had much reverence. Whether he had right on his side or no, Sir Randolph knew that he had completely forfeited it by offering the assistance demanded, saddled with a condition which he was distinctly unwarranted in exacting. He was obliged to confess to himself, painful though the admission might be, that Jim was beyond his control. He had seen nor heard nothing

from that contumacious young gentleman
since their stormy interview ; he had
probably obtained the money he required
in one of the ways he had declared open to
him, but at all events it was very clear that
he was not likely to make submission.

But though he might bully and sneer at
his wife, his daughter was another matter.
She had no idea of sitting mute, and bowing
her head to the storm. When Sir Randolph
commenced one of his bitter tirades against
Jim, Sara invariably raised her voice in her
brother's behalf. She declared that mar-
riages in these days in this country were no
more made by parents than in heaven, and
distinctly gave her indignant father to
understand that she intended to exercise
her own judgment in this matter. Upon
this occasion the girl's championship of her
brother had carried her a little too far. She
gave the exasperated Sir Randolph an
opportunity of retorting that it would be
ample time to discuss the subject, as far

as she was concerned, when there should
appear a probability of her being called
upon to decide for herself; as far as he
was aware, there was no imminent danger
of that at present.

Sara, quick-tempered and energetic, bit
her lips at her father's sarcastic speech. She
was not the girl to trouble her head because
she happened to have no suitor for her
hand. She was young, full of life and
spirits, and could afford to wait; still, it is
hardly in woman's nature not to be stung
by a taunt of this description. As may be
supposed, Sir Randolph and his daughter
were by no means drawn closer together
through these constantly recurring skir-
mishes.

As for Lady Hawksbury, she bore her
husband's continued attack and sarcasm
with all the serene indifference peculiar to
her nature. The Dowager declared she
could never be in earnest about anything,
and the Dowager was so far right, she could

not be so for long. Her likes and dislikes,
her wishes and objections, were all evan-
escent, even her own children she was fond
of, indifferent to, and angry with at short
intervals. There was no depth of passion
in her nature; she was purely superficial
in her emotions. No uncommon character,
believe me. Men and women of this
peculiar temperament are to be met with
constantly in society, and very often impose
upon their fellows to a considerable extent.
They are like shallow lakes ruffled by the
wind; the surface is transiently moved,
but there being no depths to be affected,
the disturbance is speedily at rest. Lady
Hawksbury, as may be supposed, was much
more callous to attack than her daughter,
but even her impassiveness began to give
way under Sir Randolph's ceaseless gibes.
She was not very quick of apprehension,
it is true, and a good many of the darts
launched whizzed harmless over her head,
but still enough struck home to raise

indignation even in her usually apathetic
breast.

"You need not say anything further in
reference to my unfortunate appeal to Jim,"
she retorted one morning at breakfast, when
a shaft more maliciously winged than usual
was hurled at her. "If I made a mess of
it, as you are polite enough to call it, in
my boudoir, I should like to know what
you made of it in your study. Jim didn't
quarrel, at all events, with his mother,
Randolph. He's never entered the house
since you tried your hand at persuasion."

The Baronet's face was a picture at his
wife's retort; but Lady Hawksbury was,
if an insincere woman, by no means such
a fool as some of those most nearly related
to her deemed. Foolish in this way, no
doubt, that she was invariably feigning to
have that warm, passionate temperament,
which was the very antithesis of her real
disposition, and pretended to it so poorly

that she could impose upon no one; foolish
again insomuch that she, peculiarly easy to
be seen through and understood, was ever
for arriving at her goal by tortuous lanes
and deep-laid schemes. Still, to Sir
Randolph, Lady Hawksbury was a silly,
manœuvring woman.

There is always something peculiarly
startling to the domestic autocrat when
sudden revolt takes place in the circle over
which he has so long domineered. He
must experience the astonishment that I
presume has always been the first sensation
of the governing class in all cases of servile
uprising. That his son should decline to
submit altogether to his decrees was a con-
summation for which the Baronet was not
altogether unprepared, but that the wife of
his bosom, who had been the target for his
cynicism for more than a quarter of a
century, should venture upon caustic retort,
filled him with amazement too great for

immediate speech. Moreover, it was a retort eminently practical, and with much to be said for its justice.

"It would be as well, Caroline, if you spoke of matters about which you had some knowledge," rejoined the Baronet, with much deliberation. "That I spoke to Jim that morning about his marrying Letty Auriole, I am perfectly willing to admit; I found I was fishing in waters which you had so injudiciously troubled, it was not likely that he would look at fly of mine, I assert to boot. You had stroked his bristles so completely the wrong way, he was not in a mood to listen to advice from anyone—the result, madam, that of your own wily strategy. But when you say that has anything to do with Jim's absenting himself from this house, you mistake as usual. He and I differed upon some pecuniary matters — in fact, Jim, having exceeded his allowance, came to me for assistance, which I did not feel justified

in affording him, at all events in the first
instance. It will be a good lesson to him
to feel the inconvenience of being pinched
for a little."

A certain amount of truth in this speech,
mixed with that misrepresentation of facts
with which we are wont to lull our own
self-accusing conscience so constantly in the
ordinary affairs of life. It, at all events,
silenced Lady Hawksbury, already astonished at her own temerity. She had
never, it is true, suffered the discomfort
of perpetual money difficulties, for if Sir
Randolph had been a little wild in his
youth, he had done himself no grievous
harm in this way; but her Ladyship had
seen too much of pecuniary troubles amongst
her friends not to know that, as a rule,
men waxed exceedingly bitter when thus
brought to bay. If Jim had come to grief,
and required assistance from his father,
that they should wrangle over it was, in
her experience, no more than was to be

expected, and she felt completely extinguished by her husband's speech.

That very morning Jim Hawksbury and his sister met by appointment at Rutland Gate, and turning westwards, strolled towards Kensington Gardens.

" Now, Sara, what is it ?" inquired Jim. "I have obeyed your behest without questioning ; but, really, am curious to know ' the why' of this mysterious appointment."

" Why, surely it is obvious. I want to have a quiet talk with you. I presume you have quarrelled with papa, so it is hopeless to expect to see you at Rutland Gate."

" God bless me ! no ; we never quarrel in these days. I have had a difference with the governor about some money matters, but that's nothing. I thought I'd give him and my lady time to get over their eccentric notion about my marriage."

" It is a pity it should seem so eccentric to you, Jim," replied his sister, quietly ; " because she's a girl that any man may be proud to win. No!" she continued, hurriedly, "don't be nervous; I am not going to urge it, for one moment. I wanted to question you about this feud with papa; but, as you say there is none, thank goodness there is no more to be said upon that subject."

"Nothing," replied her brother; "if Sir Randolph makes himself out-of-the-way unpleasant next time we meet—well, I shall keep out of his way for a little. I can't be in his way for long, you know, for now I am appointed to Sir Richard Bowood's staff I must be off to Canada in two or three months, of course."

"What a nice thing it is for you, Jim, and how kind and clever of grandmamma to get it for you."

"She's an unlimited trump," observed Jim, *sotto voce.*

"By-the-way," remarked Miss Hawksbury, carelessly, "did you ever see anything more of your Burnside flame? Let us sit down here. She was a Canadian, was she not ?"

Jim's temples flushed slightly, but Sara was so absorbed in the management of her parasol at that moment that she did not observe it.

" Oh yes," he replied, " I have seen her several times in town since we got to Aldershot."

" Lately ?" inquired Sara, with a slight interrogative raising of her eyebrows.

" No, not very lately," rejoined Jim, with as much indifference as he could manage to put into his voice.

" Do you admire her as much as you did ?"

" Quite ; she's very pretty."

" Ah ! you must show her to me some day."

" I shall be only too delighted," rejoined Jim, with a comical glance ; " whenever you think you can spare the time."

" Oh, I am at your service any morning

or afternoon. She walks in the Park, I presume ?"

" No, not just now. She is living rather far out of town."

" Ah well, I can wait till she comes back. Jim, don't bring me back a Canadian sister-in-law."

" Good heavens ! what put that into your head ?"

" You admire this lady more than you are wont to admire ladies generally, you see. I think it probable you will find her sisters as fascinating as I have been told men do find them. I would rather you married an English girl, that's all."

" How you do rave about matrimony," retorted Jim, bitterly. " I don't suppose it matters much whom we marry, as long as she is what society calls eligible. Marrying for love is clean out of date in these times."

Sara Hawksbury eyed her brother with undisguised astonishment. Some three weeks back, at all events, he had appeared to hold very different opinions, not, perhaps, contemplating marriage as a thing that it was necessary for him to think about just then, but very decided at all events that the lady so strongly suggested to him by his parents would not suit as a wife, much as he esteemed her in any other light.

"I am not urging anything of the kind upon you," she said at length, "but you seem to have changed your opinion somewhat since mamma spoke to you about Letty."

"Should you like me to marry Letty?" he asked dryly.

"No, I think not now. I'll own once the thought was very dear to me, and it might perhaps have come to pass if no one had interfered in the matter," replied Sara, gravely.

"Do you think she would say Yes if I asked her?"

"I am sure I can't tell. I should think not if you asked her in your present mood. Letty is too quick-sighted not to under-

stand whether a man seeks her hand in
earnest or simply conventionally."

" It does not much matter after all
whom one marries," said Jim, meditatively.
" Family arrangements are, perhaps, the
best thing to follow on this point."

Sara Hawksbury was simply utterly non-
plussed by her brother's reiterated remark.
What could he mean—did he intend her
to understand that he was now willing to
marry Letty Auriole if he could, and, if so,
what had wrought this marvellous change
in him. She did not know what to say,
and, in her bewilderment, simply ejaculated
" Jim ! "

" Yes, I know what you are thinking
about," he replied quietly ; " that it is very
odd I should have manifested dislike to
this idea not a month ago, and now should
have changed my mind. I don't say I
have altogether, insomuch as it is not clear
to me that I need concern myself about
anything of the sort at present. Still, I

recognise this fact, that Letty is a girl who is not likely to wait long for a husband, unless she lists. Secondly, she would be a wife I could esteem and like."

" Not love, Jim ? " inquired Sara, in a low voice.

" What has that to do with it ? " inquired her brother, impatiently.

Miss Hawksbury made no reply; she could not understand this extraordinary shift of ground in a man's views, and yet she began to have some hazy inkling of the truth—an inkling so undefined, at present, that she could not possibly put it into shape. It went no farther than an imagining that something rather serious must have happened to Jim. Could it be that this money scrape was of considerably vaster dimensions than he chose to admit, and that it made a wealthy connection a matter of vital importance to him ?

" I think it possible it may have a good deal to do with it," she replied, after a little, and looking her brother intently in the face.

"You don't mean that Letty would expect rhapsodies from me, do you ? "

"Not exactly rhapsodies, but I think it likely she would require to be satisfied of a man's love before she said him Yes," rejoined Miss Hawksbury.

"Then you wouldn't advise me——"

"To try and convince any woman, not an absolute fool, on that point, just now, Jim," interposed Miss Hawksbury, sharply. "I don't know what has happened to you, but I give you fair warning, my brother, if you go a-wooing in your present mood, the woman who takes you will do it because she may think it will be a profitable specu- lation in days to come. Now take me home. You may rest quite easy about my not promoting a marriage between you and Letty."

"All right, come along," said Jim, rising. "You needn't be angry, Sara. It's better

left alone, perhaps ; not only in Letty's
case, but altogether, I daresay."

" Most decidedly in Letty's case, unless
you take infinitely more trouble than you
seem disposed to do.   She's not a girl,
remember, to whom your Highness has
but to throw your handkerchief."

Jim shrugged his shoulders, and made
no reply.   It was not likely that his sister
could understand him; he hardly understood
himself.   Neither men nor women do under
similar circumstances, and more weddings
take place from simply pique than the
world wotteth of.   Sore and angry at
having been, as he conceived, made the
mere puppet of a finished coquette in his
first serious entanglement, Jim was ready
to consider love a mockery ; why, then,
should he not soothe his *amour propre*
and please his family by taking Letty
Auriole to wife ?

CHAPTER IV.

THE Knights of the Golden Circle—as the Canadian branch of that tag-rag-and-bobtail association, known elsewhere as the "Fenian brotherhood," thought fit to denominate themselves—in the meantime were getting impatient to practically show their sympathy with their oppressed brethren at home, by striking a blow which, as they eloquently and vaguely expressed it, should make "the tyrannical Saxon trimble." It certainly might be urged that, supposing they had any organisation, or ever could have any chance of successful rebellion, the time had come. The States

swarmed with lately-disbanded soldiery,
many of the more lawless of whom showed
a distaste for settling down into orderly
and peaceful citizens ; the getting back
into the groove of steady industry, by no
means of an alluring prospect to these
unruly spirits. If this political fraud, en-
titled the Fenian conspiracy, possessed any
vitality at all, now was the time to exhibit
it. The numerous subscribers demanded to
see something for their money ; insisted, in
short, that the show should begin. The
Fenian chiefs had confined their organisation principally to the collection of funds
—organisation extremely comprehensive in
that respect—but had not, so far, thought
it necessary to go farther. But some of
their subordinates, conspirators of that
grade who do not enjoy the incalculable
advantage of appointing their own salaries,
thought also that a rapid, well-planned raid
across the Canadian frontier might be profitable, without being dangerous. Man must

live ; and prices in New York still smacked
of a war tariff. It would be well to re-
plenish empty pockets by thrusting their
hands into those of their next-door neighbours.

Government, perfectly informed on these
points, and estimating the storm rightly as
considerably of the tempest-in-the-teapot
nature, still thought it might be prudent
to hurry out the reinforcements they were
about to send, and further hinted to Sir
Richard Bowood that the sooner he took
over the Canadian command the better.

Great was the exultation of Mr. Cherriton
when he heard that not only were the —th
Hussars under orders for special service in
Canada, but that distinguished corps was
to embark, horses and all, forthwith (as
Mr. Holms would say—whoever heard of a
cavalry regiment embarking without their
horses?—absurd to record such a fact). Mr.
Cherriton was jubilant past conception ; he
began to talk Western from that moment ;

he guessed Europe was played out, yes, sir, and trusted the other side would "pan out" more satisfactory. He didn't know much about Fenians, but there were grizzlies and moose and deer to hunt at all events; salmon to be caught if the Knights of the Golden Circle proved shy; duck-shooting, sleighing, skating, curling.

"By heavens!" exclaimed Mr. Cherriton, "it's from the dust-bin of England to Paradise; from charging nothing in the Long Valley to the annihilation of a scorpion brood of malcontent Americanised Hibernians. Let me at 'em, gentlemen, I repeat; transport me across the ocean, and only let me at the whole crowd—Fenians, grizzlies, moose, or beaver; in the meantime bring me a cigar, and—yes, a soda-and-brandy, Davis. Active service, my brethren, creates both thirst and excitement."

The Chirper is right, there is a fever taint in the blood on the eve of a campaign, whether it be against big game or against

our fellow-creatures. It is more or less the
gambler's excitement, with higher though
less degrading stakes. They are playing
for acres, or funded moneys at the outside;
these are setting their life upon the cast,
and unless brain be cool and nerve be
steady, may throw out for ever the first
time they trickle the dice across the board.
Jacta alea, but when the foe or wild beast
keeps the table, to throw deuce-ace is to
throw out past recovery.

Jim Hawksbury, too, catches the excitement; it would be odd indeed if he did not,
for Sir Richard's eye sparkles at the idea
that he may have work to do at last. It
has been a sore feeling to him for years
that he never has chanced to see active
service. He can by no means complain of
promotion, or of not having received his
due share of the spoils of the profession;
but in times when most men of his standing had seen sharp fighting somewhere,
he felt it seemed almost a stain on his

reputation to have been so persistently out of it.

Sir Richard had been undoubtedly dashed somewhat when he heard at the Horse Guards what was required of him. He was to keep order, protect the frontier, but most especially not to fight. Such was the summary of his instructions. Peculiarly pleasant injunctions these to carry out, for a man who never having seen active service would, of course, be sensitive to the imputation of being a non-fighting commander. How much the mutterings of the Crimean army concerning the reticent use made of the cavalry after the Alma had to do with that magnificent blunder, the "charge of the six hundred," is a thing difficult to estimate. But Sir Richard argued that it looked as if matters would get beyond temporising and protocol-writing, and that necessity would apparently arise for sharp and decisive action, which would be brought to a conclusion of some

sort almost before the telegram informed the
British authorities it had been undertaken.
A trifle cooler it may be, but not much
more to be trusted than Lieut.-General
Bloomingdale, after all—this courtly, diplomatic soldier, who had never seen a shot
fired. It is better to leave frontiers to the
protection of a rural police than to hand
them over to the army, with instructions to
confine themselves as much as possible to
bluster. "Running a man in " would constitute a somewhat undignified *casus belli*, to
be always atoned for besides by his release ;
but the death of a citizen, that is another
thing. The death of a man has led to
somewhat portentous results before now, and
is a step there is no retracting from.

Jim, catching the enthusiasm of his chief,
begins to believe that he really is embarking
for " the real thing," and looks upon himself
as thoroughly committed to a campaign as
Mr. Cherriton, indeed more so, for that
gentleman's ideas are so extremely hazy and

variable, with regard to the foe he is about
to encounter, that it is by no means easy
to ascertain whether he regards the whole
affair as a gigantic picnic, expedition after
big game, or war with America. The
Chirper's ideas of his peculiar mission are
as uncertain and changeable as the barometer. Sometimes he appears to consider
himself charged with the suppression of the
elk and the Indian, at others with the re-
establishment of the Southern Confederacy,
while ever and anon he alternates between
winning the Montreal Handicap and the
delights of sleighing by moonlight. No
very rational or consecutive talk to be got
out of Mr. Cherriton just now, so absorbed is
he in trying heavy rifles with miniature
shells and spherical balls, or useful "platers,"
with some little aptitude for jumping.

"Mr. Cherriton, my lady," announces the
Dowager's footman, one brilliant August
afternoon, at the extreme orthodox hour for
calling ; and that usually nonchalant, but at

present somewhat bewildered, cornet of horse duly follows his name.

"Delighted to see you, Mr. Cherriton," says the old lady, as she rises to receive him. No manner of use to tell Lady Hawksbury that her age entitles her to dispense with such ordinary courtesy. She deliberately refuses, as yet, to admit either age or infirmity, and decidedly is justified so far in the negative. "Not your farewell visit, I trust, although of course I know that, like Jim, you are bound for the West almost immediately."

"Yes, we are off almost directly, I am told. Going up the St. Lawrence and down Niagara. No, I don't mean that exactly, but we are going to 'where mighty Missouri rolls down to the sea,' as the song says, and to see how he does it, I presume. Beg pardon, Miss Auriole, but I didn't see you over in the window at first."

"Don't apologise, pray," laughed Letty. "You know we are always glad when you

can make time to call upon us. Like true
women, grandmamma and I have a craving
to see much of people who may be heroes
before many months are over."

"The fighting part of the affair is perhaps
dubersome," replied Mr. Cherriton, with
much gravity; "but Lady Hawksbury," he
continued, turning round to the Dowager,
with whom he was quite quick enough to
know he was an established favourite, "there
is no denying the fun of the thing."

The Chirper had paid many a visit in
Park Lane since Jim first brought him there
to lunch, and had always received a cordial
welcome from both ladies.

"How so?" inquired Lady Hawksbury.

"There's the sport, if there's nothing
else," replied Mr. Cherriton, confidentially.
"What shall I send you back, Miss Auriole?
Don't you think the claws of a grizzly bear,
the scalp of a Dakota chief, a moose's head,
and three or four brace of canvas-back
ducks would make up a good basket?"

"Stick to the canvas-back ducks, and never mind the rest," cried the old lady. "Practical people, Letty and I; we prefer substantials to trophies."

"Such a difficult country to stand up in in the winter-time," remarked the Chirper, with a semi-grin on his countenance.

"How so?" inquired Letty.

"Because," he replied demurely, "after much research into the customs thereof, I have come to the conclusion the inhabitants pass a good deal of their time either on skates or snow-shoes. It's all very well, of course, when you are acclimatised—hem! but when I put on skates, my anxiety to see what I am standing on leads to my getting down perpetually to see. Snow-shoeing, I am told, is like walking about on exaggerated rackets. I put on the latter in my own room the other day, and am bound to confess tumbled about as much as it was possible in the time."

"Accomplishments, these, Mr. Cherriton,

that require learning," said Lady Hawksbury.

"Of course," returned the Chirper, "in every life some falls must come, no doubt; some days be dark and dreary, as somebody beautifully expresses it, but it's natural in a skating and snow-shoeing country the falls should somewhat exceed the average. Still, I'm not to be cowed by bumps, Miss Auriole."

"Not you, Mr. Cherriton," cried Letty, laughing. "Grandmamma and I shall expect to welcome you back, something like Joseph, in a skin of many colours, but triumphant."

"I suppose you are very busy getting your outfit for Canada, Mr. Cherriton?" remarked Lady Hawksbury.

"Well, I am, and I am not," replied the Chirper, gravely, "it's rather hard to know what one had better take out, and what not. I was talking to a fellow the other day, who was very decided about it. 'Don't you be humbugged,' he said, 'I know the country thoroughly—was out there for years. Take out nothing but saddlery and sovereigns. You'll make money on both your gold and horse-trappings—everything else you'll get better and cheaper out there;' but, unluckily, I found out later on he thought it was India I was going to."

"And was, consequently, no authority on Canada," interposed Lady Hawksbury, laughing.

"Not in the least," replied Cherriton. "Said he believed it was rather cold there in the winter, and he should recommend me to wrap up well, and wear a respirator."

"No, no," cried Letty, "you don't mean to say anyone ever said that to you?"

"Indeed I do, Miss Auriole, and it happened just as I tell you; and now I must say good-bye. Remember your promise, please. I assure you I consider my future interests are committed to your hands."

"What does he mean, Letty?" inquired the Dowager, sharply.

"Mr. Cherriton, grandmamma, is chivalrous enough to believe that the interest of our sex is of importance sometimes to men in his profession, and I am pledged to exert myself in his behalf if ever I have the chance."

"Why, bless the boy! I beg your pardon, Mr. Cherriton—you will excuse an old woman's *lapsus linguæ*; but how did you come by that idea? You're right, you know. Take a worldly old lady's advice, and keep the women on your side through life if you can, and believe me it is not difficult. A certain amount of attention and deference will ensure the votes of most of us."

The Chirper laughed as he shook hands. "Thanks for your encouragement, Lady Hawksbury. I only hope, when you have taken proper care of Jim, you will remember there is another poor cornet of horse whom it would be charity to look after a bit also."

"Good-bye," replied the old lady, gaily. "There's no knowing what Letty and I may do for you before we've done. Meanwhile, sir, we pray you qualify yourself for high command;" and the Dowager swept Mr. Cherriton so stately a curtsy as almost to discompose that imperturbable hussar's gravity.

"Letty, my dear," said Lady Hawksbury, as Mr. Cherriton descended the stairs, "we must put him down on our list for promotion, and I think we are not quite without interest with the Canadian Commander-in-chief that is to be. What do you say, child?"

But Miss Auriole deigned no reply, unless a smile and a slight deepening of colour could be deemed such.

CHAPTER V.

MONTREAL was all alive with the war fever
when Sir Richard Bowood and his aide-de-
camp landed there in September. Very
much on fire the Canadians at that time,
taking energetic steps to arm militia and
volunteers, and turning out in veritable
earnest to repel any filibustering raids across
their frontier. The Government were quite
awake to the delicacy of the situation,
thoroughly aware that a rupture with the
United States would be a very serious thing
for the colony. Let England, as England
was, and is bound to do still, fight for the
Dominion with all her strength, yet it is

Canada that will always be in the van of such quarrel, as it may be well hoped now we never may see; people by no means so hopeful on that point in the days of my story. The States at that time were something, as Frederick the Great described himself at the close of the Seven Years' War, "like a dog that has fought, still busy licking their wounds," but casting sullen and angry glances at a power that they deemed had acted no friendly part to them during their own terrible struggle. It was only too likely they might resent any embroilment with the Canadians without investigation or dispassionate inquiry, and there were plenty of adventurers of all kinds who could see much profit in the promotion of such a quarrel. Notably it was much to the interest of the Fenian brotherhood that it should be brought about.

But there is a dash of the French blood, and a pretty strong one, flowing in Canadian

veins; and if it were necessary to call out
volunteers and militia, if there were more
regulars quartered in the two provinces than
had been the case in years gone by, so much
the greater reason for gaiety, argued Montreal, Quebec, and Toronto.   Sir Richard
and his aide found Montreal at its brightest
and gayest when they took up their abode
therein.   Jim, however, had not been installed many days in the St. Lawrence Hall
before the telegram from Father Point gave
notice that the *Star of the West* was in
the river, and on board that ship, as Hawksbury very well knew, were his old com-
panions-in-arms.

How pleasant it will be, he thought, to
have the old lot once more within hail.
This staff business is all very well, and of
course I ought to consider myself a deuced
lucky fellow.   It was wonderful good of
" the gran " to work it for me, and it may
improve as one gets on, but at present
there's no disguising it—it's cursed slow.

Then he thought of that talk with Sara in Kensington Gardens, and mused much over what she had said. He had placed too much faith in her knowledge of Letty Auriole to hazard that proposal he had so nonchalantly discussed; but it was a curious instance of how contradictory is human nature, that he, who had never seriously contemplated a union with that young lady, felt somewhat piqued at the intimation it was past his power to bring about. In short, what he had previously never dreamt of now became a thing to contemplate, at all events. But one glorious October day in that delicious fortnight or three weeks, known as the Indian summer, which prefaces the first chill blasts and wild whirlings of the wind that herald the winter—when the foliage of the woods is all ablaze with green, red, brown, and yellow, when you have bright sun and just the least touch of crispness in the balmy air; one of such days as one feels it to be imperative to be out

in, when to be chained to desk, writing-
table, or indoor occupation is a source of
much bitterness and heart-burning—the
news came to the St. Lawrence Hall that
the *Star of the West* was within sight of
the city.

Hawksbury hurried down to the quays,
and in a very few minutes was shaking
hands with his brother-officers.

"Something like a river, this, Jim," said
Mr. Cherriton. "I haven't seen how
'Mighty Missouri rolls down to the sea'
as yet, but if it beats the St. Lawrence, the
Americans have some cause to brag about
it. This is the biggest thing in 'rolls down
to the sea' I've seen, so far."

"It's a splendid panorama at this time of
the year," chimed in the Colonel, "and, as
the Cornet says in his peculiar shibboleth,
it takes a grand river indeed to beat the
St. Lawrence."

"Any news of our Fenian friends?"
asked Cherriton.

"No; I don't think there's much danger of anything beyond a small filibustering scrimmage, at all events; but you needn't be nervous, Chirper, you'll find lots of fun going on. There's plenty of society—rackets, boating, fishing, driving—though, I'm told, the real fun of the fair don't begin till the first snow. Lots of good fellows to know, and here and there a very quaint one. Wait till you see my friend, Campbell Macgregor; if he don't astonish your youth and innocence, 'write me down an ass,' that's all."

"What a tremendous Scotchman. Rob Roy and McCullum More rolled into one!" exclaimed Cherriton.

"A character, eh?" inquired the Colonel.

"Yes, you are both right," replied Jim; "although, I'd bet a trifle, of a kind you never yet pictured to yourself."

"No?" said the Colonel, interrogatively.

"No; you never, either of you, saw a French Scotchman, did you?"

"Good gracious, no!" cried Mr. Cherriton; "tell us all about him?"

"Not a word more at present; you will meet him for certain in the next few days, and will own, at all events, he's more Scotch than any Scotchman you ever met. He's more Scotch than an Irishman in a Highland regiment, and that's saying a good deal."

"Well, when one thinks of Tom Mahoney, of the 42nd, it is," said the Chirper, meditatively.

"When are they going to land you, Colonel?" said Jim.

"Daybreak to-morrow. Slinging the horses, of course, takes time; but we shall be all comfortably installed in barracks by noon."

"I must be off now," said Hawksbury. "There are rooms, as I have already said, for all the lot of you at the St. Lawrence Hall, and you'd better put up there till you are settled. We are not yet. The Chief

can't find a house to his mind. I only hope,
when he does, he won't expect me to live in
it. I'm new to the collar, of course, but,
Chirper, this staff work savours to me
a wee bit of always 'wearing the belt.'
Good-bye."

Mr. Cherriton shook his head meditatively
as his chum departed.

" He ain't right," muttered that precocious
young gentleman to himself, " and it is not
altogether this staff work that's the matter
with Jim ; he's never been himself since his
flirtation with that Lydon girl. I never
saw her, but suppose she was something a
good bit over the ordinary run for looks
and so on. She is a Canadian. I wonder
whether he's heard anything about her since
he's been out here ? However, it is a big
country, and perhaps he may never come
across her after all."

Mr. Cherriton is quite right; it is a big
country, but it has, as yet, neither the big
cities nor swarming population of the British

Isles. The centres in which men herd are so far not very numerous, and the discovery of the whereabouts of friends and acquaintances much easier than it would be at home. Hawksbury knew that the Lydons lived in or near Quebec, and, without direct inquiry, is already aware that they have returned to their home. He has seen a picture or two of the artist's exposed for sale in a shop of the leading Montreal bookseller, and a desultory question or two has told him this much. About meeting them again, Jim feels some uncertainty as to his desires; upon the whole, perhaps, he thinks it would be wise to abstain from seeking to renew the old intimacy. The impression that Lydon is a practised gambler has rather deepened in his mind of late, although he still tries to believe Clarisse ignorant of her father's malpractices—best, he thinks, that he should come across these people no more, for he is most thoroughly awake now to the feeling with which he regards Miss Lydon.

The —th have settled down into their quarters, and are plunging wildly into all the mysteries of the fur trade, ordering, with a view to the forthcoming winter, hideous head-dresses that they will never wear, and as yet understanding no further difference between black fox and astracan other than that the former looks prettiest— requisite they should settle a furrier's bill or two to arrive at a proper comprehension of the value of skins.

Mr. Cherriton is wandering vaguely up St. James's Street one fine October morning, seriously exercised in his mind, because the dashing head-dress he had ordered and just received had been pronounced, by an experienced friend, " Capital minx fur, my boy, but for pattern, damme, it's of the country, very. That's the style of cap your jolly old Cunack farmer wears, but society (including the soldiers) goes in for something a good deal smarter in cut." Now, Mr. Cherriton had thought that cap destined to somewhat astonish Montreal. He begins to have doubts about his sleigh, buffalo robes, and all the other appurtenances he has provided himself with in anticipation of the winter campaign. Moodily musing over these things, he suddenly runs up against Jim Hawksbury.

" Had it a bad night at loo, or what's the matter with it ?" inquired the aide-de-camp, laughing. " What are we looking so straight down our nose about, eh ? "

" It's all very well for you to grin, Jim, but here's a young Polar bear as has ordered his trousseau all wrong. Devilish warm, you know, and all that sort of thing, but not fashionable."

" Never mind the fashion, you'll set it when once they know you. Come and lunch at Dolly's. I'm expecting a friend. I think he'll amuse you."

" I'm on," rejoined the Chirper, curtly.

Dolly's, the well-known chop-house of

Montreal, was an imitation of the famous City establishment of that name in London. It rejoiced in a sanded floor, and those queer portioned-off pens which were known as "boxes" to our ancestors. Coffee-rooms of this description wax scarce in these days. You may see a very modernised edition of that sort of thing at The Criterion; you may see the veritable reality at The Cock, and doubtless elsewhere, but the old coffee-room box has pretty well faded away, a part of that very visionary abode of comfort about which Shenstone sang, though that anybody ever does take his comfort in an inn at the present time is a circumstance concerning which one feels somewhat sceptical. Passing through the long, narrow, dingy room, where thirsty toilers diligently gave themselves up to lunch and the understanding of sundry alcoholic puzzles, for which the place was famous, Jim led the way to a sanctum at the far end, entered, rang the bell, and inquired if Mr. Campbell MacGregor had been there ?

"Yes, sir," replied the waiter; "he begged you would not wait lunch, and said he should be back again in something like ten minutes."

"All right, then, bring it in at once," rejoined Hawksbury; "we won't wait, Chirper. I'm going to introduce you to the spruce partridge and a black duck. The partridge is a matter of taste, but I'll guarantee the duck."

They had hardly sat down, when the door opened abruptly, and a slight, sharp, vivacious man, of about forty, entered, exclaiming :

"*Mon cher* Hawksbury, I apologise that I am a little behind the time, but the business, you know, we must attend to him."

"Let me introduce you to a brother-officer of mine," said Hawksbury, as he shook hands; " Mr. Cherriton—Mr. Camp-bell MacGregor."

"Ah, you have just arrived. You have come at the right time, that is, if you like the amusements of my country. I mean, of course, the country of my ancestors. Ah, *milles bombes*," he continued, rubbing his hands; "we shall teach you to skate, to curl, and what 'whisky on the ice' mean."

"I shall be delighted, I'm sure," replied the Chirper, "to devote my attention to all three; the latter, at all events, I have, at times, studied in my native country."

A warning gesture from Hawksbury checked Mr. Cherriton's badinage, or else that young gentleman felt powerfully impelled to draw out the new comer, who he, of course, recognised as the tremendously Scotch Frenchman, of whom Jim had told them on board the *Star of the West*.

"I shall hope to see you in Quebec next week, Monsieur Cherriton," said MacGregor. "You must know I live there, and that the

General and my good friend the Captain are coming up to have a look at the ancient city and its surroundings. Ah, we are going to have great times. We shall show you the Falls of Montmorenci, there will be dancing, picnicing, and all sorts of diversion. You will do me the honour to dine, I hope, and taste the sheep's head—dish of my country, you know."

Mr. Cherriton bowed, and murmured he should be but too happy if he had the opportunity.

" Well, you have, Chirper ? " chimed in Hawksbury, " for the General told me to look out a couple of fellows from the garrison, who were good to come up as unpaid aides. That means leave, travelling expenses, and being in the thick of it, with almost nominal duties. Will you come ? "

" Will I not ! " cried Mr. Cherriton, jubilantly. " I never quite understood the advantages of the staff till now. An extra aide ! that's what I was born for, what I

came into the service to do. Tell Sir
Richard I'm good 'to stump' the whole
Dominion with him in that character."

"Ah, then I shall see you with Monsieur
Hawksbury, and have the honour to introduce you to the whisky ponche, as we
brew him in Argyleshire, eh?"

"Certainly, moosoo," replied the Chirper.

"My name is MacGregor," rejoined the
other, somewhat tartly.

"You must excuse Cherriton," interposed
Jim, quickly; "he is labouring under the
impression he is in a French colony, and
that he really understands and talks that
language."

"*Mon dieu*, sir; about Toronto you
will find there are men who speak the
Gaelic—the speech of the MacGregors!"
exclaimed the little man, drawing himself
up, while his eyes positively sparkled.

"I shall trust to quaff the punch of
the MacGregors next week," replied Mr.
Cherriton.

"Ah *bon!* good! ha, ha! we will have many tumblers of toddy together, and now, gentlemen, I must say adieu. I have to catch the Quebec boat. *Un petit verre de whisky* to our next meeting."

The dram was quickly brought and tossed off. Mr. Campbell MacGregor pressed the hands of his companions effusively, and then dashed off to the steamer.

"Well, he is a rum 'un," observes Mr. Cherriton, sententiously.

"Yes, and don't you make the mistake again of seeing an atom of French in his composition. You'll drive him wild if you do. Recollect he's Scotch—Scotch to his finger-nails ; that he will drink neat whisky, which makes him cough, instead of light claret, which he infinitely prefers ; that his foot is on his native *tapis*, and that his name is MacGregor."

CHAPTER VI.

THE FUSILIERS "AT HOME."

SIR RICHARD BOWOOD's visit to the old capital of the Canadas was, however, postponed for some few weeks. Rumours of filibustering parties on the frontier were rife, and a dash across the border in pursuit of plunder on the part of the Fenian brotherhood seemed only too likely. Partial, very, this organisation to the acquisition of real property, nor likely to be troubled with moral compunctions about the exact manner of acquiring the same. Goaded, too, by its enthusiastic subscribers to give them some sort of show for their money, and a bank could be sacked and an em-

broglio at the same time created between
Canada and the States, the more adven-
turous leaders of the brotherhood argued,
with slight risk to those members concerned
in the attempt, and with considerable
benefit to the association generally. The
plundering of a bank is always dear to
the mind of the mob; not yet instructed,
like the more educated of the criminal
classes, about the difficulty of negotiating
stolen notes, bills, bonds, and other securities;
believing also that in the interior of all
such establishments, the gathering of actual
gold and silver is akin to the gleaning on
the historical property of Mr. Thomas Tidler.
All these flying reports detained Sir Richard
at his head-quarters; there was little fear
of an invasion in strength, but it was a
very extended line of frontier to guard,
and a few hundred raiders might do much
damage in a very short time if not promptly
encountered and dealt with, to say nothing
of the possible complications with the

Government of the United States should there be *trop de zèle* in their chastisement.

October had gone, and the first snow descended in its fine feathery flakes before Sir Richard and his staff took the cars for Quebec. There was ice in the St. Lawrence, and the country was clothed' in robes of innocence.

> Every pine and fir and hemlock
> Wore ermine too dear for an earl,
> And the poorest twig on the elm-tree
> Was ridged inch deep with pearl.
>
> From sheds new roofed with Carrara
> Came Chanticleer's muffled crow,
> The stiff rails were softened to swansdown,
> And still fluttered down the snow.

Bright, clear, sharp weather, anon hazing over, as if turning to dense fog, and then the soft, white, powdery flakes came fluttering down, and though as yet the Montreal neighbourhood was barely carpeted, the papers told of quite a foot of snow on the crest of Point Diamond. The steam ferry,

however, was still running—it is not till
the ice gets thick in the river that these
tough little boats abandon their vocation
to the *voyageurs* and their dug-outs, as the
solid canoes of the St. Lawrence boatmen
are called; and Sir Richard, accompanied
by his suite, descending from the cars at
Point Levi, embarked for the opposite head-
land. The gaudy, glittering, tin-cased roofs
of Quebec are now decorously shrouded in
the cerements of winter, or, to speak more
correctly of the mirth-loving little capital
(it must ever be the historical capital), I
should say in the bridal robes of the *jour
de l'an*, for Quebec treats its five months'
snow as by no means a serious matter; on
the contrary, it is not till it has fairly
bedecked itself in ermine that the quaint
old city abandons itself to unrestrained
merriment. In the summer it is oppressed
with contrition, heat, and thunderstorms.
The two latter account for the former, and
it is possible to be very penitent about

nothing in sultry weather. As a matter of fact, I think I have seen more penitence evoked by the extremes of the barometer than the prickings of conscience. We wax sad over our shortcomings both in the fogs of November and the electric caprices of July. The cynic who pronounced remorse and indigestion synonymous terms, spoke not altogether without reason.

As they step on to the quay in the Lower Town of Quebec, a tall, blond, muscular man, attired in dark blanket coat and a plucked otter cap, pushes through the crowd and exclaims, in hearty tones :

"How are you, Hawksbury ? Glad to see you, Cherriton."

"Let me introduce you to my chief," rejoined Jim, as he shook hands. "Captain Troughton, of the —th Fusiliers, Sir Richard."

"You will find your rooms all right, sir, at The Clarendon, and I have carioles here to take both yourselves and baggage up. Here's my fellow, Hawksbury ; just show

him one of your people, and he'll pilot them
and the portmanteaus, while, if you'll allow
me, I'll do guide to yourselves."

A few minutes' tough wrestling with the
hill on the part of the sturdy Canadian
hacks, and they turn into John Street,
whirl across the deserted market-place, past
the Jesuit Barracks, enter Lewis Street, and
pull up at the door of the Clarendon Hotel
—quite the West End, this, of the ancient
metropolis, and the house relatively answering to its former namesake in Bond Street,
much as Russell's Hotel, at the foot of the
hill, might compare with The Langham.
The hotel was on the *qui vive*; Troughton
had ordered rooms for the party in compliance with a missive from Hawksbury,
and it was not likely that so important
a personage as the General Commanding-
in-chief should fail of receiving fitting
reception.

"I've a handful of missives for you, Sir
Richard," said the Fusilier, when they had

been duly ushered into the sitting-room. "The Colonel bade me say he would pay his respects to-morrow morning—that's our official hope that you will give us the honour of your company at mess to-morrow—that's ditto from the riflemen up in the citadel—that's a . card for yourself and staff to our 'At Home' on Friday, and you won't miss that, Sir Richard, if you want to see the flower of our Quebec beauties. We have some worth looking at, I can assure you, and on my soul, sir, I'd not let any of your personal staff unsworn to celibacy attend. If they are dangerous to look at, they're positively fatal to talk to."

"And yet he's walking about," muttered the Chirper into Jim's ear.

"How do you manage to take care of yourself, Captain Troughton?" rejoined the General, laughing.

"My terrible weakness, where a woman is concerned, is my safeguard," replied the

Fusilier, unblushingly. "I fall in love with em by battalions, and ask them to marry me by companies. My failing is so well known here, that a girl thinks no more of saying Yes when I ask her to be my partner for life than she does to assenting to be my partner in the Lancers; and what's shameful, Sir Richard," returned Troughton, with a comic grimace, "they pay about similar heed to the importance of the engagement."

"Well, we must endeavour to be present on Friday, and trust to save ourselves now we are sufficiently cautioned."

"You really will see some very pretty girls, and, I trust, pass a pleasant evening. Anything more, Sir Richard, I can be of use about?"

"No, thanks; much obliged for all your trouble. Hawksbury will let you know about all those cards for dinners, &c., in the morning. Good-night."

It is Friday evening, a clear, crisp, star-

light night, and you could have almost read
the papers by the light of the moon in
Lewis Street. The merry tinkle of the bells
is incessant, as sleigh after sleigh whirls on
silent runners to the dingy entrance of the
officers' mess, where the floor-cloth, a by no
means brilliant lamp, and a couple of smart
non-commissioned officers in gray overcoats,
faced with astracan fur, announce that the
gallant Fusiliers are entertaining the town.

The low carriages pull up, and from
under rugs and buffalo robes, dainty
figures, swathed in "clouds," mantles, and
wraps, with feet protected by moccasin and
over-boots, emerge, and trip gaily up the
half-dozen steps. As they turn into the
cloak-room on the right to throw off their
outer garments and shake out their flounces,
the regimental band rings out the " Ante-
room Valses," and with sparkling eyes the
fair demoiselles of the West button their
gloves, take one last look in the glass, and
then plunge into the fray. When Quebec

goes dancing, Quebec means it. Canada girls all dance, and, unless he be singularly dull, disagreeable, or misanthropic, are apt to see that the stranger within their toils shall also be at least that much instructed. Ah me! it would be pleasant to put Time's clock back some twenty years, and be instructed once more upon this point, but alas! the Liverpool lurch, the Boston drop, the Whitechapel kick, and other similar refinements, are difficult to achieve when you have set up the gout, and adopted Buxton or Harrowgate as the shrine at which your devotions are due.

In due course Sir Richard Bowood, accompanied by his personal staff, climbs the short, narrow stair, and enters the ball-room. No great decorations—a few flags and bayonets, the removal of the carpet and furniture, with the waxing of the floor, has sufficed to transform the mess-room of the —th into what, if not a pretty ball-room, is at all events a very excellent dancing-room,

and both townsfolk and garrison seem
resolved to make the most of it.

Troughton and his brother-officers, as
may be supposed, took good care that their
guests should not lack introductions. As
for Mr. Cherriton, he threw himself at once
into the thing with a will, and was leaning
against the wall in a state of some exhaus-
tion from desperately attempting to execute
a galop at an impossible pace—the order
to the bandmaster, with some regard to
supper arrangements, had been briefly,
" Play them down "—when Mr. Campbell
MacGregor slapped him upon the shoulder,
and exclaimed : " Welcome to Quebec, *mon
ami* ; we shall teach you to curl, and in the
meantime we will 'tak' a right guid willie-
waught, for old lang syne.' *N'est-ce pas?*"

" Certainly, moosoo—I mean Mr. Mac-
Gregor. I don't quite know what a willie-
waught is, but I suppose he's of kin to
' John Collins ' and all the rest of the
family. Come on, my Highland patriarch,

for I've a thirst it would be sinful not to gratify."

The pair adjourned downstairs to the refreshment buffet, and slaked their calcined throats, as Troughton phrased it, in a copious libation of claret-cup. Much badinage took place between the Fusilier and MacGregor on the subject of curling; and it was arranged that Troughton should find a team of soldiers to play the civilians as soon as might be.

"Don't you make any mistake, laird" (he always called Campbell MacGregor by this *sobriquet*, and was a prime favourite with that eccentric individual in consequence), " I'll get my men together for Tuesday— meet on the ice at eleven—whisky and sand- wiches at two—play till five—stakes, beef and greens, a curler's dinner, for which the losers pay."

" Hooray ! what you call it ? Ah, done ! *Ma foi, mon Capitaine*, I shall find a rink to beat you."

"Good—we shall see ; but mind, the soldiers will die hard."

" Ah, we shall see ; we shall see you also, Monsieur Cherriton."

" Well, I'm just about to begin," replied the Chirper.

" Ah, then we drink him's health. Here's prosperity to curling. Haigh ice, inside turn and one's stone on the tee."

Mr. Cherriton tossed a bumper off briskly to this mysterious toast, with no more idea of its meaning than if it had been couched in Sanscrit—a mystification in which I fear, for the present, many of my readers will participate.

Jim Hawksbury, returning from supper, re-enters the ball-room, and is about to plunge into a vaise, when his eyes meet those of Clarisse Lydon. Jim stops for a second, and receives a laughing nod of recognition, but at that moment there flashes across his mind all those terrible misgivings that had so oppressed him the other side of

the Atlantic. It was sheer derision that the
gambler's daughter should recognise him
again in such fashion. Did she deem him
still blind to the fleecing he had undergone?
did she suppose that he had not discovered
that her father was a professed gamester, and
she herself a veritable daughter of Circe, who
piped for fools for her sire to devour? His
first feeling was one of astonishment at her
insolent *hardiesse* in venturing to recognise
him at all. His second was to return her
salutation with the most frigid possible
inclination of the head. He could see the
astonishment depicted on her mobile features
for a moment, but she quickly drew herself
up, and during the short time she remained
seemed perfectly unconscious of his presence.
That she danced much and had no lack of
partners, Jim, watching her furtively and
jealously, had ocular demonstration; that
Troughton, and others of the best men
in the room, were keen candidates for her
hand was also patent, but she never vouch-

safed another glance in the direction of
Mr. Hawksbury, thereby leaving that gentleman, as is usual in such cases, in a state
of much discomfort and uncertainty. What
would the man have? She had greeted
him gaily, and he had shown a disposition to
ignore their former intimacy—a disposition
in which she had most readily acquiesced,
and still the dragoon was not satisfied.
Young men in Jim Hawksbury's state of
mind are a little hard to satisfy, and the
queen of the time being can make them feel
the bit pretty sharply if she list.

But quadrilles have disappeared from the
programme, the room begins to thin, and
valses and galops wax quicker as the night
goes on. The dance is evidently drawing
to a close, though still some desperate
revellers cling to the programme—would
see it out, indeed, if they had their will—
valsers these, thorough and guileless, who
would gladly dance the night out at any
time on biscuits and soda-water—who ask

no more than a good floor and a good band
—who can dispense with the flesh-pots,
and do not believe that supper and dry
champagne in profusion constitute a good
ball. 1 suppose it does now; at all events,
we don't dance much in these days, and in
time, perhaps, may emulate the civilisation
of the East, and have it done for us.
Rumour says now that it is so in shooting,
and that " a loader " is expected not only to
shoot, but to *shoot straight* with the third
breech-loader.

The final galop comes at last, the time
gets quicker and quicker, and at last
even the best goers find they cannot stay
more than thrice round the room at the
pace. Once again has the order come to
the conductor of the band from the
rulers of the revel to " Play them down,"
and he does. You may be smooth and
fast as an express train, but the music
calls you to be yet a little quicker. It is
just that extra few seconds in the mile that

settles us all, both men and horses. We last very well at our own pace, but the trifle of extra exertion hammers in the nails with a vengeance. The band soon kills the ball, and there is much helping on with wraps and moccasins at the entrance of the cloak-room almost immediately.

"Not bad fun, Chirper, our 'At Homes,' are they?" said Troughton, as they run up the steps again after packing their late partners snugly in the sleigh; "but come on now to the ante-room. We always have a symposium to finish up with—piano going, no end of harmony, tobacco, and soda, with its accompaniment."

When they entered the ante-room it was crowded. The smoke wreaths from a good score of cigars hung in heavy clouds, while above the babble of tongues rang out only the report of the bursting cork of aerated waters and the accompaniment of "John Peel," which an engineer officer crashes boldly out on the piano. Suddenly comes a cry of "Silence for the song; silence for 'John Peel,' gentlemen!" and in a moment the room is hushed as the grand old hunting lyric is trolled out by the maestro at the instrument, the whole congregation joining in the chorus emphatically, if not tunefully.

As for Mr. Cherriton, he not only expressed his unqualified opinions of the whole proceedings, but contributed his quota to "John Peel" to the utmost of his ability.

"Now, Mr. MacGregor, this is what I call snug, deuced snug and gentlemanly, you know—no noise" (you might have heard the chorus of "John Peel" anywhere within the city walls).

"Do you not think, *mon ami*, that the smoke him a little thick? By Gar, I find this cigar more strong than I think *bon*. But no matter, we shall have a great curling match this week. You no curl! Ha! we shall instruct you."

"Right you are," rejoined the Chirper;

"I'm going in for that, skating, tossing the caber, and all the sports of North Britain."

"Tossing the what do you call him? Ah! I don't think I know that," rejoined Mr. MacGregor. "Are you sure that's Scotch?"

"Highland down to your boots—I mean brogues. No; damn it, that's Irish—trotter-cases. No; down to whatever's Scotch for boots, you know."

Captain Troughton's song—"Slow are the Winter Months."

"Silence, if you please, gentlemen," exclaimed two or three voices.

Once more the room was stilled, the Engineer crashed out a few chords, and the Fusilier plunged into a well-known song of those days.

Air—"Under the willow she's weeping," &c.

Slow are the winter months gliding away,
   Whist and écarté we're playing;
Just one more tumbler and just one cigar,
   Whilst just for one rubber we're staying.

Sad, sad, kings not to be had,
Cards they are always refusing ;
Sad, sad, it's really too bad,
The long odds so constantly losing.

Slow are the winter months gliding away,
In spite both of curling and sleighing ;
We are sick when we think of skates and the rink,
And for spring and green fields we are praying.
Snow, snow, still falls the snow,
Nipping, frost-biting, and freezing ;
Snow, snow, still falls the snow,
Sciatica, coughing, and sneezing.

Slow are the winter months gliding away,
O'er hunting and shooting we're musing ;
This might do in its way, if they'd double our pay,
And of leave there was never refusing.
Snow, snow, still falls the snow,
Nipping, frost-biting, and freezing ;
Snow, snow, still falls the snow,
Sciatica, coughing, and sneezing.

Slow are the winter months gliding away,
New Year's visits we're all of us paying,
Which means getting merry on lashings of sherry,
And shocking " turns over " in sleighing.
Snow, snow, still falls the snow,
Though compliments of the season we're
wishing ;
I'm sick of your balls, of skating, of falls,
Treboggining, tommy-cod fishing.

There was considerable applause upon the conclusion of Troughton's song—not very much in it, but it possessed two points that rarely fail to hit, namely : a catching air, and it dwelt upon subjects well understood by its audience. Make a jest of some well-known social misery, put it to a taking tune, and that means a successful comic or buffo song. The fun waxes fast and furious —chaff and story go round, and more than one good song is sung, the which we have not space to chronicle. We must fain sum up in the words of the Chirper, who, when the shutters being thrown open, the faint November daylight glistened into the room, and he topped up with a cup of strong coffee, pronounced oracularly that "Her Majesty's —th Fusiliers had a very sensible notion of a pleasant evening."

CHAPTER VII.

"THE ROARING GAME."

JIM HAWKSBURY muses much over the appearance of Clarisse Lydon. Whatever he might think of his feelings towards her, though he had lulled himself into the idea that he had quite overcome all weakness regarding her, yet her mere presence had sufficed to dispel all such illusion. He had steeled himself not to speak to her, but Jim felt ruefully that it had been a resolve which had cost him dear. It would have taken much persuasion to induce him to propose to Letty Auriole now, although he had well-nigh nerved himself to inflicting such wrong on the heiress but a few weeks back—indeed, but for Sara's clear-headed counsel, might have experienced the further mortification of finding such proposal appraised at its true value and declined. He makes stealthy inquiry concerning Miss Lydon, and finds that she is quite in society, though going out somewhat capriciously; voted, indeed, one of the reigning belles and best valsers in a city where the ladies all valse.

"I don't know why," said Troughton, "but she's rather difficult to catch. She's an extremely pretty girl, and as nice as she's pretty; but she don't come to half the things she's asked to. Her father never goes out, but still it can hardly be difficulty about a chaperon. There are plenty of people would do that for her, and we are not quite so strict on that point as they are at home."

"I suppose she goes to the rink," remarked Jim, in a nonchalant manner.

"Not very often—she's a very pretty

skater when she does show; but of course
we've plenty of them. Quebec girls can
all skate and valse—born with these two
accomplishments, I believe. Meanwhile,
you'll be at the Latimers' dance on Monday
and next day, old man; you'll have to see
myself and three other soldiers do battle
against 'the Laird' and his merry men on
the curling-rink."

"Is he a good player?" asked Jim.

"Yes, capital; only sometimes, to prove
his Scottishness, he will drink neat whisky
at lunch. He simply can't; and if this
match is going against us, I shall just get
the Chirper to give us a lift. The Laird is
immensely impressed by Cherriton, I can
see, and if the Chirper goes in for being
Scotch after the sandwiches, is quite capable
of taking 'willie waughts' neat, to an extent
that will make his play erratic for the next
hour or so."

Hawksbury grinned as he replied: "I
don't think you could give the Chirper a

commission he would more thoroughly
enjoy."

"No," returned Troughton, laughin
"Let us hope there will be no necessity—

> "O a' the games that e'er I saw,
>   Mon, callant, laddie, birkie, wean,
> The bravest far aboon them a'
>   Was aye the witching Channel Stane.
>
>   O for the Channel Stane,
>   The fell gude game the Channel Stane,
>   There's no' a game among them a'
>   Can match old Scotia's Channel Stane."

Ah yes, the veteran curler's pulse
quickens when he once more hears the
boom of the "stanes" and the wild war-cry
of "Soop her up." He recalls many "a
grand shot" made in the days when his
muscles were firm and his eye was true, and
he could be depended upon by the skip to
"wick a stane" to a certainty. Most of us
look on with deep interest at those games in
which we were once past masters, but few, I
should imagine, look at the pastime of their

youths with keener appreciation than "the ancients" of "the roaring game"—men who feel, with the Ettrick Shepherd,

> They'd boom across the Milky Way,
>   One tee should be the Northern Wain,
> Another bright Orion's ray,
>   A comet for a Channel Stane.

But our curlers of to-day are not in this wise. No braves of the veteran battalion, I ween, are those men who cluster on the ice in that long, low wooden shed by the side of the St. Lewis Road this Tuesday morning. A critical observer looking them over would have said the civilians were the "fittest;" there was a suspicion of having been up all night about the soldiers, that boded ill for their performance in a game where eye and hand are specially required.

"You've got us, Laird, safe as houses to-day," cried Troughton, gaily, as he shook hands with Campbell MacGregor. "We were all dancing at the Latimers' till past

four this morning, and I'll go bail haven't
managed above ten hours' sleep amongst us.
Not one of you there; but if you don't
settle us before luncheon, look out; mine's
an afternoon team to-day."

The Fusilier was a true prophet. I suppose
the soldiers had what is technically termed
" the sun still in their eyes," for, in spite of
the pithy exhortations of their chief, they
displayed lamentable weakness and infirmity
of purpose. Their intentions might be good,
but their " stanes " went sadly wide of their
intentions in each case, and they responded
to their skip or captain's call to play up
with languid inaccuracy. Fifteen to five
stood the civilians, when the whisky, sandwiches, Hawksbury, and Mr. Cherriton made
their appearance on the ice.

" The case is desperate, Jim," whispered
Troughton. " I was just wishing for an
eclipse of the sun or whisky. Give the
Chirper his instructions. I rely upon him
to settle the Laird. For the rest, the more

whisky is consumed the better. My lot are safe to improve, while the opposing rink will probably do the reverse. We are all a little low, while the enemy are at their very best."

Mr. Campbell MacGregor, as we know, prided himself upon his Scottish descent. He was a scion of one of those Highland families whose devotion to the cause of Charles Edward had to be atoned for either on the scaffold, or by expatriation to the Canadas. Keeping some few of their traditions, they had naturally intermarried with the French inhabitants of the Lower Province, and the result had been, as in his case, the production of a race who, while speaking French and broken English, had a wondrous reverence for all the old Highland customs. Skating and curling they mastered pretty easily, but "the sport," such as moose-hunting, duck-shooting, salmon-fishing, &c., came to them unreadily, while the whisky was always a matter of tribulation to

men whose instincts impelled them to light
claret. Still, they were Scotch to the tips
of their fingers, and drank the national
liquor, although it might be with tears in
their eyes.

The Chirper gave a grin of satisfaction
when Hawksbury, in a hurried whisper,
made him acquainted with his mission.

"All right, Jim," he said; "tell Troughton
I'll see the MacGregor through willie waughts
and dochan doris's till, I'll answer for it,
' the stanes,' as you call 'em, look a little
mixed, and he's bothered to know which is
which."

In pursuance of this insidious policy,
Mr. Cherriton at once devoted himself to
" the Laird."

"Ech, mon!" he exclaimed, "but they
tell me it's a great day for the MacGregors.
Here, Saunders," he cried to a servant,
"hand across the whisky. Mr. MacGregor
and I are going to drink to the roaring game.
N'est-ce pas—that is, 'you are good for

your pint stoup, and I am good for mine,' as the song says."

" *Bon*! hooray! Here's success to curling," exclaimed the Laird, as he held out his tumbler. " *Assez, c'est assez*, my good friend," he continued to Saunders.

" Nonsense," interposed the Chirper; " up to the cuts, mon. Who ever drank a Hieland toast without the whusky was up to the cuts? Indeed, the Gordon Highlanders would wonder you could reconcile it to your conscience to mix water with it at all. Ah, that's more like," continued Mr. Cherriton. " Curling for ever!" and he tossed off a jorum of right stiff whisky-and-water.

" Success to curling," cried MacGregor, as he followed the Chirper's example.

The strength of the libation made him cough somewhat, but what mattered that, providing he conformed strictly to the customs of his ancestors.

Mr. Cherriton did his perfidious work right well, and when luncheon was declared

over and the game began again, the Laird
had taken his "ain pint stoups" and other
"stoups," under various names, to an extent
that decidedly interfered with his general-
ship.

"The borrow," which is the allowance
made by the skip for the twist of the stone,
was considerably at fault. The skip or
captain usually determines this, and calls
for the "in turn" or "out turn," on the
player's stone, much as a man might be
adjudged to play right or left side at
billiards, or receive similar directions concerning the bias at bowls. Their skip was
wild, and the civilians naturally followed
their leader's game. The soldiers had
pulled themselves together. The slight
"lowness" of the morning had been rectified
by a taste of "the crathur," they were now
playing in very different form, and point by
point stole up to their adversaries; at four
o'clock the civilians could boast of being
only three to the good.

The match was who might be ahead when the clock struck five; it being understood that another end might be started, tantamount to another "over" at cricket, as long as it was before the clock struck. The MacGregor has recovered himself by this time, and is not only curling splendidly but jockeying his side with grand judgment. It is a great fight at present. If the soldiers played wild in the early morning, and the civilians were equally loose after lunch, yet both sides are doing their best now, and rink after rink results in no more than a point either way.

It is whispered through the skating-rink next door that there is a dour fight about "beef and greens" going on upon the curling-ice, and the skaters trooped in to see the finish of the match. Dainty girls in seal-skin caps, close-reefed petticoats and plucked otter muffs, escorted by men in knicker-bockers, double-breasted shooting-jackets, and mink forage-caps, begin to crowd the

raised and boarded side-walks. This curling-rink, for the benefit of the uninitiated,
consisted of a piece of solid ice frozen from
the ground by flooding, of about one
hundred feet long by twenty broad. On
each side rose boarded side-walks above-
mentioned, being about six feet across, and
it was upon this that the lookers-on took
their stand. For the curlers, the " side in "
were all engaged on the ice. The captain
or skip stood behind the tee, ordering the
battle, *i.e.* directing the play of his men,
who all sent up their stones to the best of
their ability in compliance with his dictates.
One of these three was at the mark to play
his stones, while his two partners, armed
with brooms, stood right and left on the
ice, prepared to sweep the ice in front of
the stone or not, according as the skip
might call to them. Prompt, strenuous
sweeping often makes a difference of six or
eight feet in the run of a stone, and it is
for the skip to judge how much of such

sweeping may be required, or more profitably
altogether dispensed with. The game exactly resembles bowls, with the exception that
instead of having a movable ball like the jack
to play at, the curlers play at a fixed mark
on the ice called "the tee."

The struggle gets closer and closer. The
soldiers collar their adversaries, amidst much
cheering from their own side ; but the next
end MacGregor and his followers place a
point to the good, only to be once more
caught by their adversaries in the succeed-
ing round. The skaters have gathered
thick now, and there is a perfect hurricane
of applause when the marker calls : "Two
minutes to five, and twenty all." The game
depends upon this last end. The soldiers
lead, and their first man puts one so close
to the tee, that Troughton calls upon him at
once to lay a guard. His second stone is
well played, but a trifle slow, and the skip's
orders to "Soop her up" (*i.e.* sweep her up)
rang shrilly through the rink. She is

sooped all they know, but the soldiers are
fain to confess they'd have liked it better if
she'd run four feet more. It is the civilians'
turn now, and acting under the orders of
the MacGregor, their first man cuts away
the insufficient guard, and then lays his
second stone very close to the tee. Still
Troughton's side have the best of it, and the
Fusilier calls to his next man.

"Lay me a guard here—inside turn, and
this borrow."

The stone is well played, but, in spite of
strenuous sweeping, lacks strength. Like
the former guard, it is laid a little too low.
Called upon to lift it with his second stone,
the player puts on too much steam and
sends his first off the ice. The Laird now
calls upon his second man to wick, i.e. kiss
the in stone of the soldiers. The order is
admirably complied with ; the player drops
his stone lovingly on the top of the other,
which sends it gently a couple of feet or so
forward, remaining itself in the exact situa-

tion the adversary had previously occupied.
To guard this is, of course, the next thing
to accomplish, and the MacGregor has slight
cause to complain of his man's well-played
effort in that respect.   Still, it is not a dead
cover, and Troughton's voice rings down
the rink as he calls upon his third man to
play straight up the ice : " Wick me this
guard sharp and fine, and you'll take both
guards and the in stone out."

The shot was admirably executed, but
the player failed with his second stone,
which was delivered too strong, and, amidst
shouts of " It's roaring ! " swept past the tee
and off the ice.

The third man of the civilians now
placed two stones in, but neither of them
was very good, and it was evident that the
issue of the struggle lay between the two
skips.   Troughton played first, and curled
one beautifully up, that, twisting between
the enemy's stones, laid well inside in them,
and caused a burst of applause from the

soldiers. His second stone he played with
admirable precision, as a long guard somewhat over the line half-way up, that is
known as the hog. It was a dead cover.

"Viva Troughton!" cried Mr. Cherriton;
"you're done, Laird, this time, only one
chance for you to take his guard out this
time, and his stone next."

"Nothing of the sort; I no what you call
done by any manner of means. *Vive la
guerre!* Now, Monsieur Cherriton, I play;
I play d—n strong, and I take both his
guard and his stone out this shot."

A smile of incredulity ran round the
spectators, whilst the soldiers were already
discounting their victory.

Whizz! and without any twist either one
way or the other, MacGregor's stone met
the guard full at the pace of an express
train; it sent that picket flying with such
celerity and trueness that, striking the stone
it was intended to cover, the twain disappeared from the ice, leaving their ruthless

assailant within half a foot of the coveted tee. Laughing loudly, the MacGregor curled up his remaining stone, and the verdict was four in to the civilians and game by those points. The old curlers rubbed their hands and chuckled, as well they might, for no such shot had been played for many a year, and it's a question yet whether the curlers of the ancient city have forgotten Campbell MacGregor's famous finish for the civilians in the winter of Sixty—.

And now the rink breaks up, the skaters, like the votaries of the " Channel Stanes," abandon their recreation, and tramp back over the crisp snow in knots, or in some *cases*—strong emphasis on the substantive —in couples. Quebec adjourns to dress for dinner ; the male population, with praise-worthy intent of doing justice to such meal, not, as a rule, above fortifying themselves against the fatigues of the toilette with sherry and bitters. The drums and fifes of the

Fusiliers are spluttering out " The Roast Beef
of Old England," in Lewis Street, as some
four or five of the curlers, attired in ordinary
evening costume, run up the steps of the
Stadacona Club on the Esplanade, for it is
there the vanquished are to entertain their
conquerors, and, judging by the table,
decorated with cut-glass and flowers in
that private room on the first floor to
which the belligerents betake themselves,
there is very little *Væ Victis* likely to
characterise the entertainment. Not only
are the two contending teams about to dine,
but there are a good half-dozen of guests to
boot, and a very few minutes sees them all
mustered. Hawksbury and Mr. Cherriton,
it is superfluous to say, are amongst these
latter.

After the preliminary soup, fish, and an
entrée or two, comes the orthodox dish of
the meeting, and with exultation on his lips,
and sore misgiving in his mind, the hero of

the day exclaims : "Ah, the beef and greens,
God d—n !"

The round of boiled beef and its garnish
is a dread undertaking to Campbell
MacGregor, who has memories of fierce
indigestion brought on by similar Titanic
repasts in bygone days. To Johnson's
famous aphorism of " brandy for heroes," he
would have added, " and, *parbleu*, joints."
These curling dinners, indeed, were always
occasions of sore tribulation to the Laird,
although he would not have missed one for
the world. They involved eating heavy
joints and the drinking of strong waters,
both of which exacted fierce retribution the
next day from his foreign-cultured system.

" Snug, it's deuced snug, you know," exclaimed Mr. Cherriton after dinner, when
" the materials" were going their round.
" It's a grand game, MacGregor, a grand
game, and I'm going in for it right away.
Beg pardon, but after making such a shot as
you did this afternoon, can you *quite* recon-

cile it to your conscience to be drinking claret?"

"No, no; just a glass, you know. Hein! We come to the whisky ponch *toute suite*, what you call directly."

"Just so. Hallo, Troughton's got something to say, apparently."

"Gentlemen," said the Fusilier, who was at the head of the table, rising, "we never speechify, as you know, on these occasions. I rise to give the sole toast permitted, with which, by custom, I am allowed to associate our successful opponents. I shall say no more than that a better or more pluckily-fought match I never played in; and now call upon you all to drink, 'Beef and Greens' and the Rink that beat us."

Of course the toast was acknowledged with tumultuous applause, and the knives drummed sharply on the tables as the Laird rose in reply.

"Gentlemen, on behalf of myself and colleagues, I beg to tank you very mooch for drinking our healths. We are curlers, as our forefathers were." ("There was one of his team from Connaught," muttered the Chirper.) "We, like you, know all the games of our ancestors." ("Including cattle-lifting, arson, and treason," muttered Mr. Cherriton.) "We beat to-day, but it was one great fight, and if we played again to-morrow, fortune would probably follow you. Meanwhile, gentlemens all, we drink your good health, and, with pardonable pride, couple with it our own victory."

"Bravo, Laird, quite right," exclaimed Troughton. "That last shot of yours specially deserves drinking, although you all played like trumps. We have drunk your healths, you know, but, bless you, we'll do it again, just to show we bear no malice."

There was much inconsequent cheering and much drinking of the health of Camp bell Macgregor as a result of this speech. "Macgillycuddy of the Reeks," as Mr.

Cherriton had by this time affectionately christened him, had, under that depraved subaltern's guidance, abandoned the light claret, which constituted his usual beverage, for demoniacal tumblers of "hot Scotch," and bade fair to shortly sally forth to swear either feud or friendship with the clan McPherson, or any other "superior person."

"A song, gentlemen," suddenly exclaimed Hawksbury. "I humbly request that the chair do sing 'Canada Girls.'"

"No, Jim, I think not," retorted Troughton. "I'm good to sing, but not 'Canada Girls.' Why? Because you must all be so sick of it."

"Not at all; not a bit of it," resounded from half-a-dozen voices.

"Very kind of you fellows to say so, but if you are not, I am. No, I'll sing fast enough, but I'll give you 'The Rink' as a send off;" and, in clear mellow voice, the Fusilier trolled out the following ditty:

"THE RINK."

Air—"The Ivy Green."

You may talk of your sleighs and treboggins, et cet.,
  They are all very well in their way;
But treboggining's slow, and sleighing no go,
  In a very short time you will say.
On a cold frosty day in Canada's clime,
  The best way to pass it, I think,
And the one that best with my humour doth chime,
  Is to have a "go in" at the Rink.

    Crossing the ice as if on hot plates,
    How funny we look our first day upon skates;
    Crossing the ice as if on hot plates,
    How funny we look our first day upon skates.

That wretch, Cupid, who's lurking we know everywhere,
  And upsets resolutions and states;
Has somehow decreed that somebody's there,
  Somebody else to help on with her skates.
Then that buckle it hideth and cannot be found,
  And that strap so much looking for takes;
But some people we find from time out of mind,
  Have been slow getting into their skates.

    Outside edging and no mistakes,
    How very much better we're getting on skates;
    Outside edging and no mistakes,
    What confidence now we're getting on skates.

If you think you are safe, I should think you were "on,"
    The results of these *têtes-à-tête* mark ;
And with me you'll agree that you'd better have gone
    'Twixt two danger-boards in Hyde Park.
A friend of mine once near proposal had got,
    And a comical story relates,
How he set his teeth hard, took himself by the head,
    And threw a back fall in his skates.

        Cleverly hedged he saved his stakes,
        Insensible there he lay in his skates ;
        Bathing his temples no difference makes,
        He *wouldn't* come to that day upon skates.

The grammatical lesson there, too, to be found,
    Makes up for the bumps and the shakes ;
If adverbs are scarce, interjections abound,
    From inverted *comers* on skates.
Then squaring the circle we're quite easy in,
    When cutting indifferent eights ;
As a mercantile friend remarked with a grin,
    " There's a deal to be done, sir, in skates."

        Outside edging and no mistake,
        Could we square our tailor as well as our eight;
        Outside edging and no mistakes,
        Uncommonly good we're getting on skates.

How there were more songs and more
toasts ; how, after the party broke up, there
was a difficulty about persuading Campbell

MacGregor that he did not live in the cathedral; while Mr. Cherriton, warbling "Snow, snow, still falls the snow," fell even more quietly and continually than that insidious element, provoking Jim at last to exclaim, "I'll be shot, Chirper, if you don't look like lying as long as the subject of your melody;"—must be left to conjecture. If Mr. Cherriton had settled the chief of the MacGregors, he had also considerably settled himself. All the way home he apparently deemed himself played with the "in turn," and, after gyrating wildly, flopped tranquilly on the pavement, and then informed his companions that "Slow were the winter months gliding away." Restored to his feet, Mr. Cherriton immediately played himself with either an "in" or "out turn," and with a similar result. When he arrived at The Clarendon, he blandly threw his candlestick at the head of the "Boots," with some muttered observation about "taking a guard off;" and, when finally deposited in his bed, earnestly entreated Troughton, Jim, and the " Boots " to " Soop him up."

CHAPTER VIII.

"THROWN OUT."

IT is the week before Christmas—one of those bright but gray mornings so dear to the sportsman, whether his destination be the turnips or the cover-side. You know the sun will blink out for a little about midday, but that most of your fun will take place in that soft gray light in which birds are so good to kill, in which fences assume no unreasonable proportions, and when either hound or retriever can mostly speak to it— what hunting-men designate a scenting day. In the dining-room at Ringstone, Sara Hawksbury and Miss Auriole, arrayed in their riding-habits, are scrambling through

an early breakfast, for do not the Cottleston
meet at Bottlesby cross-roads, and has not
Uncle Robert undertaken to chaperon them
to that celebrated meet? Not likely my
lady would be down at such early hours,
while it is seldom Sir Randolph graces the
breakfast circle nowadays.

The door opens, and the Rector, clad in
orthodox Oxford gray, with his lower extremities breeched and booted, dashes into the
dining-room like a strong sou'-wester.

"Boot and saddle, young ladies," he
exclaims, in his mellow, hearty voice.
"Who'd waste time on a second egg such a
morning as this? Why, they're bound to
find if they come within a mile of a fox,
and bound to kill unless he's an undeniable
clipper."

"We won't be five minutes," rejoined
Sara. "I'll just pour you out a cup of tea
to keep you quiet while we get our hats on,
and by the time you have finished it, Letty
and I are at your service."

The Rector was in great spirits as they jogged along to cover.

"So you heard from Jim last mail—eh, Sara ?"

"Yes, and he is full of all the diversions of the Canadas. He raves about skating and curling, and pronounces it 'No end of a country to soldier in.'"

"God bless the boy !" exclaimed Uncle Robert. "Why, there's not a pack of hounds in the whole of it."

"I think Jim said something about the Montreal fox-hounds," interposed Miss Auriole.

"Well, that shows love of the thing," rejoined the Rector ; "but you can't make much of a country that is under snow all the season. Poor Jim, I pity him, or, for the matter of that, anyone else who is not on his way to Bottlesby cross-roads this morning."

"Ah, Uncle Robert," said Miss Auriole, laughing, "I understand this is one of your and Sara's days, and I may expect to lose sight of my escort as soon as they find."

"I'm under the impression hounds will go this morning, Letty; and also that Miss Lambton will be out. Under which circumstances, as you know, Sara will require a deal of looking after," rejoined the Rector, with a quiet chuckle.

"I always follow my pastor," rejoined Miss Hawksbury, gaily, as she caressed her dark chestnut; "but if Miss Lambton is getting the best of it, I'm afraid — I'm afraid——"

"Afraid what?" inquired Miss Auriole.

"That I shall have to ride my own line," was the blithe response. "I'll not be cut down by any Lambton that ever crossed saddle."

"Come, Sara, don't talk nonsense. We can't afford another family feud, and you know your blessed brother nearly broke Dick Lambton's neck and his own when they raced for the only practicable place in

that big bullfinch in Corchester pastures
three years ago."

"Jim was over first, anyway," rejoined
the young lady.

"Yes, in every sense. I never saw anybody come a prettier spread-eagle into a
field, unless it was Dick Lambton two
seconds afterwards. We saw no more of
them that day. Here are the hounds."

Many members of the hunt came forward
to greet the Rector and his fair companions,
for they are all well known with the Cottleston. The first thing to attract the ladies'
attention is a dark-blue habit on the back of
a strong brown horse, and they immediately
proceed to interchange "Good-mornings"
with Miss Lambton. The courtesy of the
duello is strictly observed in these cross-
country tournaments, and it is a pleasure, I
fancy reserved for women alone, that con-
gratulation of a rival on the condition of her
steed which in their private judgment is far
too fat to gallop.

As for the Rector, he is much exercised by the appearance of a stranger on a big bony gray—a close-shaved individual, excepting short, mutton-chop whiskers, attired in a single-breasted Melton coat, Bedford cords, and butcher boots. No possible enlightenment to be got in response to his many inquiries of " Whom might he be ? " Nobody knew. No one had ever seen him before. Still the big gray, if not a handsome horse, had a wear-and-tear look about him, and his rider sat him as a man not altogether unaccustomed to the business. But the master gives the signal, and the cavalcade jogs on to Bottlesby Scrubs, a small wood hanging on the side of a hill, and notorious as a sure find in the annals of the Cottleston, troubled, nevertheless, with this drawback, that the fox's point, upon whatever side he may break, may as a rule be put down as Beechdown Gorse, a rattling three-mile gallop, and that this circumstance is known to every member of the Cottleston.

As may be supposed under these circumstances, it was wont to be a somewhat irritating day to the master. It was not that the hunt was inundated with "tailors" from the large towns—as methinks I have heard whispered of the Cheshire and some other packs—but given a sure find, an almost certain burst in one direction over three miles of a galloping country, and it is small wonder if there be a little jealousy about getting well off. Upon the rare occasions the fox did not make for Beechdown Gorse, the huntsman and whips generally had the day to themselves, the field having been left *en masse* on the low side of the cover.

The Rector and his fair charges, with perhaps a score more, are assembled on a little knoll about two hundred yards from the south-west angle of the cover. Uncle Robert knows from long experience that the hounds generally head down in that direction, and that a view to commence with and a capital start immediately afterwards are amongst the perquisites of the situation.

" You're not to trouble about me, Uncle Robert, when they go," said Miss Auriole, laughing. " I have put myself in Mr. Normanton's hands, who knows all sorts of gates and easy places, and has a regard for my neck as well as his own."

" I'll take every care of you, Miss Auriole, never fear," exclaimed a stout jolly-looking gentleman, who must have been riding a good bit over sixteen stone. " I'm much more to be depended upon than a Hawksbury, believe me, when it comes to hounds running."

" Ah well," laughed the Rector, " it's only the weight makes you reliable, Normanton. A few years ago, before you joined 'the Welters,' your charge would have had to ride hard if she meant keeping her chaperon in view through a quick thing."

Mr. Normanton chuckled. It is a delicate tickling of our vanity to be reminded of the prowess of our youth, but when that prowess is purely apocryphal, such flattery becomes irresistible. Mr. Normanton had been a skirter from his youth upwards, and never ridden really to hounds in his life. Much knowledge of the world had Uncle Robert, and, you see, he did want Letty Auriole taken care of just now. He was, in good sooth, about as anxious that Sara should have the best of Miss Lambton as that young lady herself, and quite aware of this fact is Miss Hawksbury.

Suddenly comes a deep-throated challenge, followed almost immediately by a babble of tongues from the scrubs. But they want no lifting or hallooing to this morning; before huntsman or whips can get to them they crash through the low end of the cover, and race down the big grass-field at a pace that leaves no time for talking. They stream along mute on their errand of vengeance.

"A cracker, by Jove!" cries Uncle Robert,

as he crams his horse through a small fence which separated him from the field in which the hounds were running. " For'ard, Sara ; the blue habit's over the rail to the right."

He might have spared his breath, for his niece was over the fence a little to his left almost as he spoke. It is, as the Rector predicted, a really quick thing, and the end of the first two miles sees a great weeding out of the field. Those that can't ride, those that don't mean to ride, and those that did not get well away, are, of course, all disposed of. Similar fate is fast befalling those whose horses are a little wanting in condition, but not of these are those that come from Ringston stables, be they Abbey or Rectory. The company gets select, as may be well supposed. On the right lie the master, the huntsman, and some half-score more; on the left about a similar number, comprising the Rector and his niece, Miss Lambton, her brother, and the stranger on the gray horse, also hold their own gallantly; but it is one of those occasions upon which racers at racing weights would be put to it to live with the hounds. The first flight do their devoir gallantly, but must honestly admit that they are lying farther off than they would do if it laid at their discretion.

And now the hounds, to the amazement of Uncle Robert, suddenly swing round to the left; they had been running straight for Beechdown Gorse up to this time, but the fox has apparently changed his mind; (foxes, like men, do not always follow the lines we have prescribed for them), the result of which is, of course, to place those riding to the left on vastly favourable terms with their dapple-coated confederates. It equally follows that the farther you laid to the left the more did you benefit by this sudden shift of direction. Miss Lambton and her brother, lying wide on that side, accordingly found themselves at the head of affairs, and no two people better disposed to make the

most of the favours of Providence ever discovered themselves in front in the midst of
a good thing.

"Come along, Laura," cried Dick Lambton,
"this is luck; we've nicked in with a vengeance, and have got a clear lead of the
field."

Miss Lambton said nothing, but followed
her brother promptly, while a glow of satisfaction thrilled her veins as she thought
of a certain rifle-green habit left a good
hundred yards behind by this fantasy of the
fox.

Sara Hawksbury had as quick an eye to
hounds as anyone of her family. She saw
the sharp turn of the pack their way as
soon as her uncle, and lying slightly to his
bridle-hand, took up the new line, even
more readily than the Rector; but prompt
as she might be, there was no getting over
the fact that the Lambtons, and the
stranger on the gray horse, had recognised
the situation at sight, and were now sailing

away with a strong lead. Equally bitter
was it to Miss Hawksbury that her rival
should have the best of her, let it be by
accident or by horsemanship, and it would
have been veritably a big place that would
have made the one draw bridle, should she
see the other upon the far side. Now the
hounds twist somewhat to the right, and
it becomes evident that Beechdown Gorse,
after all, is reynard's real point; and that
his temporary deviation was probably due
to having been headed in some shape; but
the turn does not materially change the
places of the first flight. Uncle Robert,
remarking how well the stranger on the
gray horse sends him along, is more than
ever exercised in mind as to who he may
be, while his niece is wishing viciously
that she could only just get upon terms
with Laura Lambton, an equality which
that young lady shows no disposition to
share, clinging indeed to the lead with

which the fates have favoured her with admirable tenacity.

In this fashion they race down to Beech-down Gorse, the hounds bearing slightly to the right. The Lambtons, the horseman on the gray, and other of the leaders, make for the right or upper side of the cover—a proceeding in which they are naturally imitated by the master, huntsman, and others, who, thrown out to some extent by that turn of the pack to the left, have now an opportunity of putting themselves a bit to the good again.

"This way, Sara," cries the Rector, keeping away to the left or lower side of the cover. "He can't stay in the Gorse with such a scent as this; they'll carry him right through; and then the big earths at Bowtross is in his line for a hundred. We shall be a lot to the good taking this side."

Nobody ever questioned the Rev. Robert's knowledge about fox-hunting in the Cot-

tleston county. He knew every cover, gap,
and fence in it, and could always make a
very fair shot at the line a fox would take
if not interfered with : a man that would
have probably turned up at the finish if
mounted upon a hack, and known more
about the run even then than most of
those who had been with the hounds.

Of course Sara followed his lead mutely,
and then occurred one of those absurd but
provoking *contretemps* which will at times
happen to those who hunt.

Taking a pull at their horses, they made
their way, at moderate pace, to the far end
of the cover, and there, to their dismay,
discover that they had lost the hounds.
Not a sign, not a sound, not a trace of
them. It was as if the ground had opened
and swallowed fox, field, hounds, and huntsman.

The Rector, though no Puritan, was a
straightforward, conscientious parson according to his lights ; but, sad to say, a

somewhat strong and profane expression did escape his lips upon finding the result of his little bit of strategy. He made a powerful but mental resolution against "trickery," when he should be with hounds for the future, and then, turning to his niece, exclaimed :

"I can't even hear them. We're done, Sara ; they've slipped us, dear."

"Stop. Look, uncle, there's the gentleman on the gray going as if he knew all about it. Like us, he's no doubt thrown out a bit, but I should think he can see them though they are probably running wide of him."

"Of course—of course," said the Rector. "Nobody would ever be sailing along in that fashion who couldn't see them. How well the fellow goes, Sara ; it will take us all we know to catch him."

Once more the Rev. Robert takes hold of his horse's head and sends him along best pace, but the stranger on the gray is

lying rather to their right, and some three
fields ahead of them.   A stern-chase is
proverbially a long chase; but it is sur-
prising how hard it is to catch anyone with
a great start across a country unless their
horse be beaten.

The Rector and Miss Hawksbury pound
away perseveringly, but the gray and its
unknown rider, though evidently going
quite at their ease, are still not to be
come along side of.   That they are catching
him by degrees is satisfactory, and at last
Uncle Robert gives a jubilant shout as he
and Sara for the first time jump into
the field at one end as the mysterious
horseman jumps out at the other.

It is odd they see no sign of the hounds,
catch no glimpse of a red coat—nor, for the
matter of that, of any other coat—nor, what
is still more irritating to Miss Hawksbury,
of a certain blue riding-habit that, when
last she saw it, had most palpably the best
of her and Uncle Robert.

" Hang the fellow !" ejaculated the
Rector. "I never heard tell of a Flying
Dutchman in the fox-hunting line, or else
I should put that fellow down as a phantom
horseman !"

" Hush, my uncle," rejoined Sara,
laughing. "Have you not heard of the
Hartz Mountains, Walpurgis nights, and
broomsticks ?"

"Those latter are steeds with much capa-
bility of endurance, according to tradition,
and that fellow's gray is possessed of stout-
ness. It's very odd we can neither see nor
hear anything of the hounds now. He
never seems in doubt for a minute, but
sails along as if they were lying either just
in front or a little to one side of him."

" There is one thing very clear," rejoined
Miss Hawksbury ; " the fox don't mean
going to Bowtross Earths."

" No, we are going straight as a die for
Slingsby. Who ever heard of a fox heading
that way before from Bottlesby ?"

But the Rector and his niece were destined to get more astonished every minute as they slowly but surely overhauled the horseman on the gray. Neither hounds, huntsman, nor any other riders were in sight, and still this mysterious centaur urged his singular career with a steadfastness of purpose that seemed inexplicable. There was no faltering, as is so noticeable in the case of a man who is "thrown out" and somewhat uncertain about what point he shall make for. The man on the big-boned gray is sailing along across country with an evidently defined object of some sort; and yet, if he is riding to hounds, where are they? and if he is not, what can be his motive? At last the Rector gets near enough to hail him, while at the same moment the stranger becomes conscious of the steady thud of galloping hoofs behind him. He looks round, promptly draws bridle, and, raising his hat in deference to

Miss Hawksbury, inquires quietly if he can
be of any assistance.

"The hounds, sir, the hounds; where
are they?" cried Uncle Robert, breathless
with excitement.

"I really don't know," rejoined the
stranger; "they held away to the right
of that cover some two miles or so back at
a racing pace."

"Do you mean to tell me," rejoined the
Rector, "that they never went into it?"

"Certainly not. I saw that, for I was
well with them at the time; they swung
sharp past it, and, as I told you, bore away
to the right as hard as they could go."

"And may I ask, sir, what induced you,
being with the hounds, to ride in this
mysterious fashion across country and deceive your fellow-creatures?"

"I deceive my fellow-creatures?" exclaimed the gentleman on the gray. "May
I inquire how?"

"Why, sir, here are my niece and myself who are thrown out, and who have been riding our hardest the last quarter of an hour to catch you, under the impression you were with the hounds."

The stranger could not repress a low laugh, as he murmured :

"I am very sorry for the mistake."

"But what do you mean by it?" asked the Rev. Robert, irritably. "What on earth are you careering across country in this way for?"

"Because," rejoined the stranger, still struggling with repressed laughter, "I wanted to go to Slingsby."

"And what on earth made you want to go to Slingsby when the fox didn't?" rejoined the Rector, brusquely.

"The foxes and myself don't follow the same profession exactly," replied the man on the gray, smiling; "though there is but little betwixt us, according to country-

side gossip. My business is healing—theirs
stealing."

" I don't understand."

" My dear sir, I am Dr. Donaldson, of
Bottlesby, and I have left the hounds to
visit a patient at Slingsby."

The Rector's face was a study. The sell—
to use a colloquialism—was perfect. He and
Sara had simply been hunting a sporting
doctor instead of a fox.

At last Uncle Robert spoke.

" You left hounds that were running to
visit a sick person ? It was a noble thing to
do, sir. Allow me to shake hands and to
introduce myself to you as Mr. Hawksbury,
Rector of Ringstone—my niece, Miss
Hawksbury."

" I think," said Donaldson, as he bowed,
" I have had one of the family under my
charge — Mr. Hawksbury, of the —th
Hussars, was a patient of mine last year
at Burnside."

"Oh, it was you that took care of my brother?" exclaimed Sara quickly.

"I can hardly say that, for he really only wanted quiet and to be let alone," rejoined the young doctor, laughing. "I didn't interfere with Nature—that was all."

"And have you left Burnside?" inquired Miss Hawksbury.

"I have a living to get," rejoined Macdonald curtly, "and did not see my way into getting it at Burnside."

"I trust Bottlesby will prove more propitious," rejoined the young lady courteously.

"I am not going to try it. I have only taken charge of Ashford's patients for three months, he being an old friend with a sick wife, who is ordered change of air."

"Still I hope, Dr. Donaldson, we shall see you at Ringstone during your stay in these parts. I think I can guarantee you a welcome both at Abbey and Rectory; and now we must say 'good-bye,' though

I think, Sara, we must thank our friend before we go."

"For what?" exclaimed the Doctor.

"For a very tidy little run," rejoined Uncle Robert, his eyes twinkling with mirth. "May I only have as good a gallop next time I'm thrown out. Good-bye!"

CHAPTER IX.

"BRENT LODGE."

PAST John's Gate (now amongst the things that were), past John Street without, away something like a mile beyond the turnpike, stood one of those châlet-like houses which are the delight of the well-to-do classes in Quebec. It laid back a little off the road, standing in its own garden, after the manner of these villas generally; a one-storied building, with a verandah running round two sides of it.

A charming place this last to smoke a cigar, read, or indulge in idle reverie in the golden summer-time. Now, its roof ridged with snow and some slight accumulation of drift in its corners, one might well wonder what on earth was the good of it.

But Clarisse Lydon would have told you that she spent many happy days there when the St. Lawrence was one continuous glitter, when lucifers would have gone off at touch on the tin-roofed houses, when Quebec was deluged with Yankee tourists, and its inhabitants had departed to the salt waters. When the upper town looked deserted, and the dust was ankle-deep in John Street, while the lower town roared and seethed amid the sharp stirring of the business caldron therein.

It is hard to make out the place now—difficult to believe that centre grass-plat, upon which the snow lies piled, for it has the shovellings from the drive in addition to its own proper burden, is a blooming flower-garden in July—that the apparent drift to the left conceals a pretty piece of rockery.

There is no greater transformation than these Quebec villas exhibit in the change from their summer to their winter dress.

Lydon had lived at Brent Lodge now for some years—not through all Clarisse's recollection, but she certainly was a mere child when she first knew it as her home. She could remember her mother there—that dark, sprightly, semi-French woman, from whom Clarisse inherited much of her beauty and most of her quick vivacious manner. The house—or cottage would be perhaps a more accurate definition—consisted of a drawing-room and dining-room on each side of the entrance, and a couple of rooms at the back. Behind the drawing-room, on the right-hand side, is Clarisse Lydon's own room, opening out on to the verandah before mentioned; opposite is the artist's studio, with a small conservatory adjoining. Clarisse sat, the morning after that "At home" in St. Lewis Street, plunged in profound thought. Book, em-

broidery, and brush were all thrown aside,
and the mistress of the apartment had
evidently given herself over to reflection.
She had not been unprepared to meet
Hawksbury, for the papers had long ago
informed her of his arrival in Canada, on
the staff of the new Commander-in-chief.
In the last few days she had been made
aware, through the same channel, of his
presence in Quebec. That he should be,
therefore, at the dance of the —— Fusiliers
was only pretty much what she expected;
but their meeting had certainly been a
very great surprise to Miss Lydon. She
had looked forward with pleasure to resuming their intimacy on the same easy
footing upon which they had parted in
London. Hawksbury had met her gay
greeting with a frigid bow; the girl's pride
took fire at once, and she took most especial
care not to come within speaking opportunity of the Hussar during the evening.
She argued, as was very natural, that his

position on the Commander-in-chief's staff
had somewhat turned the young man's
head, and that the inflation of his position
predisposed him to drop those whom he
had known in more modest days.   Then
she reflected that though Jim had known
them intimately in Grove Terrace, yet he
had not known them in society.   Could
that be the meaning of his icy greeting,
that he shrank from acknowledging them
as intimate acquaintances before the world?
And as this occurred to Clarisse her lips
curled, her cheeks flushed, her eyes flashed,
and it was, perhaps, quite as well for Jim
that he and Miss Lydon were not destined
to come across each other just at present.

Hawksbury, as we know, has at last arrived
at the bitter conclusion that Lydon is a
professional gambler, and that Clarisse is
simply an instrument in her father's hands.
An old-world artifice this, upon which there
has been much ringing of the changes in life
—real, narrative, and dramatic.   Yet bear

with me a little, reader, and, it may be, you shall find a newer combination of Mercury and Ashtaroth than is yet known to you.

The more Clarisse meditates upon her last night's meeting with Jim the more indignant she becomes ; she twists and turns the affair in every possible light, but comes ever and again to the conclusion that she, Clarisse Lydon, as proud a girl as ever stepped, has been the mere plaything of a young man's idleness. That, pleasant as it might be to trifle with her in Grove Terrace, the Hussar had no idea of recognising her in society. " Men flirt," she thought bitterly "with girls below their own status, but do not care about acknowledging the acquaintance in a ball-room ; and Mr. Hawksbury no doubt has the presumption to look upon me in that light." And thereupon Clarisse vowed in her wrath that the next time they met no recognition whatever should escape her.

They were, to some extent, at cross pur-poses, although that hardly explains the

situation; but Miss Lydon is utterly ignorant
of the fact that their departure was too late,
and that her sire had, though with much
apparent reluctance, borne away with him
near on five hundred pounds of Hawksbury's
money. Lydon had never mentioned that
last visit of Jim's to his daughter. He had,
moreover, taken charge of a few lines of
adieu that Clarisse had addressed to her
admirer, and consigned it to the waste-paper
basket instead of the post. What was his
object in so doing? Simply this: he had
suddenly come to suspect that his daughter
cared more for the Hussar than was good for
her. Little likely, he argued, with much
worldly wisdom, that anything but disappointment would come of that flirtation.
It was a trifling wrench now, and they were
not likely to meet again; but lines of farewell are apt to produce reply, a correspondence grows up, &c. No, it was better,
he thought, for Clarisse that their connection
with the Old World should be completely

severed; and, under those circumstances, to tell that their scheme to avoid taking Hawksbury's money had failed, was not only unnecessary, but decidedly best avoided.

He lounged into his daughter's room this morning after his usual fashion; but had she not been preoccupied with her own reflections, the chances are Clarisse would have observed a nervous restlessness about her father very foreign to his accustomed absent manner. The worn face and short hacking cough showed that the Canadian winter was trying him hardly.

" Had you a pleasant ball last night ? " he inquired, after wandering about the room aimlessly for a minute or two.

" Pretty well. I have been at some I have enjoyed more," replied the girl.

" Which means, I suppose, you didn't get your fair equivalent of dancing," observed the artist, with a fond smile.

" No, indeed, I never have to complain about that. I'm not altogether ugly, papa,

and I can dance ; and under those circumstances the young men mostly take compas-
sion on us."

"Then what was the matter with your
ball?" inquired Lydon, glancing inquisitively
at her.

Clarisse flushed, and hesitated for a
moment—then exclaimed : "Why should I
not tell you—why not candidly own it ?   I
met Captain Hawksbury there, and he all
but cut me.   I am foolish enough to admit
that I was a little hurt."

" And you ? " inquired Lydon curtly.

" Was as distant as himself; but I'll own
to feeling disappointed.   Intimate as he was
with us only a few months back, I could not
have believed a slight social change in our
relative positions would have induced him to
greet me as if I were a bare acquaintance."

" The way of the world, Clarisse," rejoined
the artist, moodily.   " I think, if I were you,
I would avoid Mr. Hawksbury during his
stay in Quebec."

"I shall do nothing of the kind," rejoined the girl proudly, "although my recognition of Mr. Hawksbury will be one of the slightest in future."

"It is my express desire, Clarisse, that you should abstain from going out till the Commander-in-chief and his staff have left Quebec," returned Lydon quietly but firmly.

"Of course, if you desire that, it is another thing, and I shall comply with your wishes naturally ; but, papa, I'll confess to being astonished."

"Did you make Sir Richard Bowood's acquaintance ? " continued her father, without notice of her last remark.

"No, I was not introduced to him. He bids fair to be exceeding popular in the command. I heard only golden opinions concerning him. A fine soldier-like-looking man."

"A good-looking fellow ; yes, and a thoroughly courtly man he always was.

Dick Bowood was always popular and always lucky," remarked Lydon absently. "A favourite with both sexes, and no one ever grudged him his good fortune."

"What, you knew him, papa?" ejaculated Clarisse.

"Yes, well enough, years ago. But," he continued, "I am getting garrulous and beginning to babble about a dead past. Never heed, child, and keep what I have just told you to yourself. I have no wish to claim acquaintance with Bowood now. It would be painful for both of us, most especially for me."

"Is it because that past is so painful you never tell me of your English life, papa?" rejoined the girl softly. "I never heard you allude to it until you met Mr. Hawksbury."

"It is dead, as I told you before, Clarisse. When I first met Hawksbury at Burnside I could not resist the temptation of gossiping about a world I knew in days gone by better than he does at present. Foolish, of course; but we cannot quite resist the old memories. Yes, I am a man of two lives, the first of which lies buried; remember, for you I have only my Canadian life."

"You cannot think, papa, I wish to pry into your past. I thought it might amuse you to talk about those old times as it did in England. I felt sure I could be an amused listener," replied Clarisse.

"Odd," rejoined the artist, in his usual absent manner, "that after burying myself so many years, I should run more risk than I have ever done of being recognised by an old friend. As you know, I have ever kept clear of society, except it was purely Canadian. I have held scrupulously aloof from the garrison, and yet, certainly of late years, ran slight risk of being recognised. Now the one man who might possibly know me has come out here as Commander-in-chief. Dick Bowood was my dearest friend in days lang syne—the man who stood steadfastly by me, with two more, as long as it was possible, in the big scrape that wrecked my life. Stanch, yes, they all were ; but none truer than Bowood. It was not till I fled from the charges brought against me that he sorrowfully gave in, and refrained from further fighting my battles."

Clarisse listened with deepest interest to her father's speech; but he stopped abruptly, walked two or three times up and down the room, then suddenly exclaimed :

" But I'm idling the whole morning away with my old recollections. I wish you to keep out of Sir Richard's way, remember."

" Certainly, papa ; no great restriction, as he is not likely to stay long in Quebec."

Miss Lydon, indeed, as she pondered over her father's command, rather wished it rescinded. She felt, as she mused over Jim Hawksbury's cold recognition, that she should have dearly liked to show him that plenty of the best men in the Quebec world

were only too proud to be her partner in
the dance, or to take charge of her in any
manner; and she knew perfectly that she
could demonstrate that to him in a very
few days, only let there be something going
on, as was pretty certain to be the case
when the Commander-in-chief and his staff
were sojourning in the old capital of the
Canadas.

However, that was not to be, and it was
somewhat unlikely that she would come
across Hawksbury, in consequence of her
father's behest. If she was to avoid all
gaiety in which Sir Richard Bowood and
his staff were concerned, well, then she was
scarce likely to come across his aide-de-
camp, whether she should be in Montreal
or Quebec. The communication between
the two cities is so easy, that the
pleasure-lovers of either think little of
running up or down upon notice of gaieties
in prospect.

Then her thoughts veered round, and

suddenly Clarisse began to muse upon what
could have been the scrape that her father so
dimly alluded to. Was it that which had
banished him from England? Oh no, surely
not; he had married and settled in the province. Exactly; but then, how came he out
there? Why did he never speak of the past
—why never allude to with what object he
had come to Canada? He was an artist, he
made a moderate income by his craft; but—
and the girl had now her late English experience to go upon—artists from the old
country seldom think there is a living to be
got in the Canadas. No; it was scarce likely
her father would have abandoned London
for Quebec unless there had been pungent
and pressing reason for such exodus.

What could this scrape have been? She
wished now he had never mentioned it.
How, too, did he come to have been an intimate friend of Sir Richard Bowood? She
remembered well, in the Grove Terrace days,
questioning Jim Hawksbury about the artist-

world of London—a world that she naturally felt interested about—and how he had replied that he knew nothing whatever of it; the two professions ran in such widely different grooves that, except in rare instances, they knew nothing whatever of each other.

"No matter of not assimilating, that I am aware of," quoth Jim. "Simply as I never come across the art-world, I take it they don't often run against the soldiers."

And the more Clarisse Lydon thought over all these things the less she could comprehend them. What had been that scrape of her father's? Why did he settle in Canada? And why, yes why, did Mr. Hawksbury refuse to recognise their former intimacy?

CHAPTER X.

"NEW YEAR'S VISITS WE'RE ALL OF US
PAYING."

JIM HAWKSBURY's time at Quebec has passed
away pleasantly enough. The garrison has
done its best to make Sir Richard's sojourn
pleasant to him, and the lively city has
responded blithely to the soldiers. A
bachelors' ball, various private dances, and
other junketings have been organised by the
citizens, and the Commander-in-chief and
his staff can make no complaint that time
hangs heavily on their hands. The vivacious
Mr. Cherriton, who attends every diversion
he can hear of—curling, rinking, valsing,
sleighing, suppers, interlaced at times with a
little dash of "unlimited"—vows that five

hours' sleep is quite sufficient for any man, and that Quebec is quite competent to deal with its five months' snow, which, far from being an affliction is rather a blessing than otherwise. Mr. Cherriton, at present rather of opinion that snow and the thermometer near zero is but a barometrical sign of a convivial country, imparts to Hawksbury his opinion that "the polar bears, whales, seals, &c., spend their whole time valsing round the North Pole, and that the famous song of 'The Mock Turtle'" (see "Alice's Adventures in Wonderland") "is a slight historical error, the ballad being actually sung by the walruses in the polar neighbourhood."

Mr. Cherriton, in his indefatigable research of Canadian customs, has heard that the diversion of cock-fighting is still carried on in semi-surreptitious fashion amongst the French habitants, and the Chirper has insatiable curiosity to see that sport of former days, which advancing civilisation in

our own country has consigned pretty well
to oblivion. But though his friend Troughton
admits that it is at times to be seen in the
suburbs of Quebec, yet urges he can hear of
no tournament of such description likely to
be held at present ; and adds rather emphatically : "Don't think it is a thing, Chirper,
you will care to see twice when your
opportunity comes; and remember, if sought,
it will. Well, you will find a good deal of
rowdyism associated with the sport. Don't
be astonished if you find yourself involved in
a row to wind up with."

Sir Richard Bowood and his immediate
followers are, however, once more back in
Montreal. The general has succeeded in
renting a very nice house on the mountain,
and has opened his doors to society in right
regal manner. A man of considerable
private means and of fastidious tastes, and
recognising thoroughly that his position
called upon him to entertain, there was
slight cause for supposing that things would

not be handsomely done at Flodden House ; and they were. A big dinner and a little one every week were standing orders in the establishment. While the notables, military and civil, of Montreal were duly feasted at the first, it was to the latter were bidden the prettiest girls and the pleasantest people. The first, it was well understood by the garrison, meant uniform or excellent dinner, but a not particularly lively evening. At the latter, the officers had been given intimation that plain clothes were more acceptable ; and the more youthful of the garrison perhaps more often circled the table than their seniors. Sir Richard, with all his Old World courtesy, dearly loved genuine sociability. He duly respected the obligations of his position, but thought it no harm to gather round him a pleasant set of people, although their social position did not claim official recognition at his hands. Jim Hawksbury found the winter months gliding away by no means slowly.

As for Mr. Cherriton, he simply declared
he'd never a moment to himself. "I'm a
philosopher, Jim, I *are*," observed that
young gentleman, with a solemn waggle of
his precocious head; "and I tell you what it
is—life in Canada is a succession of falls.
I upset myself twice yesterday sleighing;
cannoned against an ice-cart for the first,
and did not allow for 'the slew' at a sharp
turning for the second. I came down three
times in fifty minutes in the skating-rink;
tumbled over my broom curling in my
enthusiastic endeavours to 'soop her up;'
went a moral cropper at whist to the tune
of twelve pound ten, due to pursuing the
noble game on the top of unlimited champagne; and hang me if the 'carter,' as they
call the cabmen in this country, didn't con-
trive to upset me as I betook myself home
from 'the gunners' mess,' to finish with——"

"Drunk, I suppose," said Hawksbury.

"Well, when I left him he was apologising
to the lamp-post, and imploring it to keep

its right side in future. I suppose he'd been doing 'Bourbon straight,' as they call it, more or less; I should say more muchly. But, I say, Jim, you and I are going New Year's visiting together, you know; and New Year's Day is next Tuesday."

"Cannot help it," replied Hawksbury. "I shall have to be here. Sir Richard, of course, is obliged to receive."

"Just so; I forgot that. Never mind, we'll prance round with our respects, &c., on Wednesday. I'll bring the chestnuts over and drive you."

"All right. You're not to empty the sleigh more than once, mind."

"Well, that leader is just a leetle awkward," rejoined Mr. Cherriton, grinning; "but it isn't eighteen inches to roll out; nobody ever was hurt by being upset in a sleigh."

The famous New Year's visiting of the Western hemisphere has been described from every point of view; and I should imagine few of my readers are unacquainted with, at all events by hearsay, the ceremony of "sitting up"—Canadian vernacular for staying at home to receive.

"Compliments of the season," says you; "No use unless you drink it," says they;— was the terse and graphic way in which one narrator described it.

Is there not the famous skit by Newall, describing the New Year's visiting of "The General of the Mackerel Brigade?" who, from tendering the compliments of the season, arrived gradually at "looking severely at his pocket-handkerchief, and trying to leave the room by the way of the fireplace"—to "going under the table like a stately ship foundering at sea, and requesting the wine-cooler to tell his family that he died for his country."

The fashion seems to be rapidly extending to our own land. Already Christmas cards are rife ; and *les étrennes*, that terrible un-recognised tax of our lively neighbours, bids

fair to become an institution in England.
Are we destined to be the double victims
of Christmas Day and *le jour de l'an*? The
imposition of a new social tax is so easy;
the abolition of an old one so hard. Do we
discover that our bills are less at hotels
because attendance is charged in the bill?
Do our friends' domestics yield gratuitous
service when we are their masters' guests?
No, indeed. I heard not long ago a story
of a butler who gravely asked his master
for an increase of wages, on the plea that
he entertained so little, the perquisites were
below consideration!

On that appointed Wednesday, however,
Mr. Cherriton duly makes his appearance
at Flodden Lodge with a tandem of rather
weedy chestnuts.

"They're not much to look at, Jim,"
observed that gentleman, in reply to his
chum's somewhat disparaging glance at the
turn-out; "but they can go. These things"
—here he pointed to his sleigh—"are no

weight, and I did a mile with them in a
little over three minutes the other day."

" You did ! They don't look like trotters."

" Bless you, no ; they are nothing particular in that line ; but they gallop tidily
when I can get a clear stretch to put them
along."

" All right, young 'un," said Jim, as he
slipped beneath the buffalo robes, " only
just mind it *is* a clear stretch before you
introduce me to that performance."

The chestnuts were not really a bad team,
although they evidently preferred doing
their work in an easy canter ; and the
Chirper and Jim got very satisfactorily
through a considerable number of visits.
At last they elected to make a call some
three miles out on the Dorchester Road—
a good straight road and with plenty of
room in it. Mr. Cherriton put the chestnuts
along, and they galloped their three miles
in a trifle under the quarter of an hour,
whirling past the few vehicles they met or

overtook with wild and jubilant cries. At
last they near the cross-road, down which
the people they intend to call upon live.
With some trouble the Chirper pulls his
horses into a trot, and they turned the
corner in sober fashion. But the blood of
the chestnuts is up from their mad gallop,
and fretting and fidgeting, they give their
master plenty to do to keep them in hand.
The road, too, is now narrow—only just
possible for two sleighs to pass, while the
drifted snow on either side lies deep.

"Oh Lord, Jim, here's a go !" suddenly
exclaimed Mr. Cherriton, still further check-
ing his impetuous steeds, the effect of which
was to make the leader still more volatile
in her conduct. "Another sleigh meeting
us—ladies in it, too ; so we must try and
draw up to let them pass. If they'd been
all men I'd have driven at 'em and chanced
it. Carlotta looks like standing, don't
she ?"

This was the fractious leader, now

showing much disposition to pirouette on
her hind legs.

As before said, the road was narrow. It
was not only that, but a raised causeway,
with sloping banks running down to the
fields on either side. On these slopes the
snow had accumulated, so that it was impossible to have guessed they were not
pretty well level with the roadway by
anyone not conversant with it. Both
Mr. Cherriton and Hawksbury knew well
to get off the beaten track was to plunge
into a snowdrift some twelve or fourteen
feet deep. This did not exactly mean
danger, but it meant a thorough turn over
and considerable breakage of shafts and
harness, in all probability; an inconvenience
to be avoided, if possible.

"Nip out and get to her unruly head,
Jim!" exclaimed Mr. Cherriton anxiously.

Hawksbury threw back the buffalo-robes;
but it was too late. The approaching sleigh,
a family vehicle apparently, and drawn by

a pair of horses, was already alongside
Carlotta ; that fractious animal reared and
turned about to make one tremendous bound
down the bank.

" Pull, Jim, pull this near rein for goodness'
sake !" cried the Chirper vehemently, at the
same time doing his own possible best to
drag their volatile leader round. But they
only half succeeded; the mare's forefeet came
down over the edge of the bank, and, as
might have been expected, upon finding
herself getting into deep snow, she plunged
furiously forward, dragging all behind her
into the drift, which presented a confused
scene of struggling men and horses to the
occupants of the other sleigh, the driver of
which, having first whipped his horses past
the catastrophe, had pulled up. He was an
elderly gentleman, accompanied by three
ladies, of whom one was middle-aged, the
other two young.

The upsetting of a vehicle in the snow
countries is generally ludicrous to witness.

There is slight fear of injury to any of its occupants; and the affair is always looked upon in a humorous light. As Jim Hawksbury struggled out of the drift on to the hard track, still clinging to the rein of that refractory leader, he could not resist bursting out laughing at the luckless Chirper, who had been shot so completely down the slope as to have had to abandon his hold of his horses, and who presented for a second or two nothing but his legs to the spectators. A few frenzied struggles, during which the snow is convulsed and appears like a drift in the pangs of delivery, then Mr. Cherriton having once more succeeded in getting right side uppermost, presents his well-powdered face, and begins struggling out of his embarrassment. Deep snow is not quite so bad to get out of as an Irish bog. You do not sink usually more than about halfway up the thigh, and the Chirper had not above five or six yards to fight through; but it is astonishing and somewhat absurd to see the helpless wallowing and plunging it involves.

"Keep still, sir," cried the old gentleman, "for one moment. Jump out, girls; take out the cord and throw it him. I always drive with a bit of line in the sleigh in case of accidents."

Thus adjured, Mr. Cherriton ceased to struggle, and waited to see what was going to be done for him. The two girls sprang from the sleigh; produced a bit of strong clothes-line from beneath the seat, of excellent substance for splicing broken shafts, &c.; and throwing one end to the Chirper, said merrily, "If you catch hold we will draw you out." Quite awake to the value of the assistance now is Mr. Cherriton; he lays hold of the cord and is easily drawn to firm ground by the young ladies, who laughingly congratulate him upon the rescue, while the old gentleman regrets he should have been the unlucky cause of the mishap.

"But bear a hand, girls. You are neither of you afraid of horses. See if you can't give a lift down below."

Mr. Cherriton looked hard at his fair assistants for a moment, and had a vague suspicion that the taller he had seen before. But it is difficult to recognise a lady in her furs and enveloped in "a cloud," as the light knitted scarfs worn round the head and dropping like a veil across the face, are called. Moreover he had scant time for investigation, as it was evident that Hawksbury stood in much need of assistance with the horses. Jim had got the fractious Carlotta on to the track again; but though he had run up the rein and shortened his distance from her considerably, he had not as yet got to her head.

"Catch hold of her bridle, Chirper," he exclaimed, as that gentleman joined him, "and make her draw the other out. I'll look after the wheeler as soon as he gets his feet on the road; and as soon as they have pulled the sleigh out, too, we'll take stock of damages."

The two girls were following Mr. Cherriton with undoubted laughter on their lips; but as Hawksbury spoke, the taller stopped abruptly, handed the cord which she was carrying to her companion, and said, in a low tone, "Go on and offer them this if they want it. I'm going back to the sleigh. I have reasons."

"But, Clarisse, it will look so odd. Do come. Why on earth should you not?"

"Do as I tell you," replied the other in a vehement whisper. "I have reasons, I say. You shall know all about them the minute we're once more under the buffalo-robes. Now go on quick, Madeline;" with which peremptory command the young lady turned abruptly and walked back to her uncle, leaving the further rescue of the shipwrecked Hussars to be carried out by her cousin, Madeline Maschereau.

Under Jim's directions the overturned

sleigh was quickly drawn out, and it was soon ascertained that they had come much cheaper out of their capsize than they could have ventured to hope for. The Chirper's harness was new, and so stood considerable strain. A broken shaft really seemed to be the only serious damage, and that, thanks to M. Maschereau's timely supply of line, it was not difficult to splice. Miss Madeline superintended the operation with great interest, and laughed and chatted freely with the two gentlemen over their misadventure ; holding, indeed, the fractious though now sobered Carlotta for some minutes when the mysteries of splicing required the joint energies of the ship-wrecked ones. When the tandem was once more pronounced in working order, Mr. Cherriton escorted the young lady back to her sleigh, thanked M. Maschereau for his courtesy and assistance, and wound up with :

"My name is Cherriton ; trade, cornet of

—th Hussars. I should like very much to know to whom I'm indebted for—for—for rope, and who the young ladies are who so kindly drew me out of that abominable drift."

"My name is Maschereau," replied the old gentleman, laughing. "Shall be very happy indeed, Mr. Cherriton, to see you at 24, Sherbroke Street, if you will do me the honour to call. The ladies who went to your assistance are my niece and my daughter. I trust you will get home without further misadventure—adieu."

The Chirper made his salaam; received a laughing little nod from his late assistant, and a much more stately bend from her companion, then turned to rejoin Hawksbury, who was holding the horses.

"Well," said Jim, as Mr. Cherriton took his seat and once more resumed the reins; "did you make out who our friends were?"

"Yes, Monsieur Maschereau, of 24, Sherbroke Street. Does that enlighten you? His niece and his daughter were

the two demoiselles who came to succour
our afflicted selves. Does that tell you
anything ? "

" Yes. Maschereau I've heard of as a
leading merchant in the city, and that is
about all I can recollect concerning him.
On Sir Richard's visiting-list, I know ; but
I don't think he's ever as yet honoured us,
though I'm pretty sure he's been asked to
dinner."

" She's rather nice, the young lady,"
observed Mr. Cherriton.

" Which," inquired his companion—" the
niece or the daughter ? "

" There you beat me," replied the Chirper.
" I don't know ; I mean the one who held
Carlotta while we spliced the shaft. Deuced
odd. I couldn't see her very well, but I
seem to have a hazy idea that I ought to
know who the other was—that I've met
her before. She's rather a striking figure
and manner."

" I think we'll give up this call," said

Jim, "and as soon as you get a good open place to turn them in, go quietly home, eh ?"

"All right, there's lots of room a little farther on."

Their struggles in the drift had reduced the chestnuts to sober manners ; and having been turned round, they proceeded on their homeward journey in a steady slinging trot. Mr. Cherriton meanwhile was un-usually silent, and apparently immersed in thought. Suddenly, as they neared Montreal, he exclaimed : " By Jove ! I've got it, Jim. I can't say whether I'm right or wrong, but I can tell you now who the taller girl reminded me of—that Miss Lydon, whom I saw and was just introduced to at the Fusiliers' dance at Quebec."

" Clarisse Lydon ! " exclaimed Jim.

" Exactly; and if I don't make a mistake, Clarisse is what the other called her as they were pulling me out of the drift. I didn't dance with her because she was engaged, Heaven knows how deep—but she was the most striking girl in the room; and though I forgot all about it afterwards, I recollect being puzzled at the time, knowing her well, as you do, that you should throw such an advantage away as you did;" and as he concluded, Mr. Cherriton glanced with some curiosity at his chum.

"Well, you might guess, if you remember the écarté business," replied the other. "I never even spoke to her at Quebec, and have rather regretted it ever since" ("rather" was a very considerable qualification of his real feelings on the subject). "Still, if you are right, Miss Lydon is Monsieur Maschereau's niece, and I'm sure to see her shortly."

The Chirper nodded assent.

CHAPTER XI.

VERY curious is Hawksbury concerning M. Maschereau, his belongings and antecedents; but there is little more to be learned about him than Jim already knew. M. Maschereau is a cadet of a tolerably good French Canadian family, who, like many others, began life as a clerk, got on and blossomed into a merchant—a thriving tolerably well-to-do man of that class, and much respected nowadays. Mr. Cherriton is allowed no peace till he avails himself of M. Maschereau's good-natured speech and calls in Sherbroke Street. That Jim accompanies him it is needless to observe; but upon the whole Hawksbury hardly considered the visit a success. They saw only Madame Maschereau and Mademoiselle Madeline ; and, although the Chirper pronounced the latter "an awful jolly girl," when they regained the street Jim had not felt carried away altogether by her mother's somewhat commonplace conversation. In the interests of his chum, Mr. Cherriton had asked pointedly after Mademoiselle's cousin ; but the curt answers to inquiries showed too plainly that Madeline had her instructions on that point.

"Sorry for you, Jim," observed the Chirper as they left the house. "I've done what you told me, but it isn't much good. That I am right about it's being Miss Lydon, of course I've ascertained ; but as far as my lights go, I should say she doesn't mean to see you — why, it is for you to determine. Miss Madeline would laugh and gossip fast enough about anything save her cousin—touch that point, and our conversation became terse past all conception."

"I must see her," muttered Jim; "I played the fool at Quebec—idiot, beast, that I was."

"I say," said Mr. Cherriton, "you'll excuse me, but you must be pretty bad, Jim, to go on in this way. I don't want to be indiscreet, but if you're in real earnest and *must* see her, why I'm bound to stand by, Jim. I'll manage it."

"How?" inquired Hawksbury abruptly.

"Pooh!" rejoined the Chirper, with an air of inflated self-confidence, "I can easily worm everything out of that little Maschereau girl."

Here Mr. Cherriton's conceit was abruptly extinguished by a roar of laughter from his companion.

"My dear Chirper," said Jim, "don't you fall into such an egregious mistake as that. The little Maschereau girl, as you call her, will, if she hasn't already done so, turn you inside out at your next visit. It requires a very much cleverer man than you or I to pump a woman, and something else besides."

" What ?" inquired Mr. Cherriton laconically.

"A tolerably foolish woman to operate on."

" Well, never mind, Jim ; all I mean is, I'm good to do the best I can for you. Now look here, I'll call for you to-morrow morning at seven sharp.   There's a sporting friend of mine thinks he's got a horse good enough to enter for this great Montreal Trotting Sweepstakes, and he wants just to rough him up for a mile in a lightish sleigh —a cutter, you know, though not a racing one—just to see what sort of time he can make of a mile.   He'll drive the horse, and I want somebody to work the stop-watch."

" I'm your man.   You call and I'll be ready.   I turn off here.   Good-bye."

" He is, by Jove," murmured Mr. Cherriton, as he walked away, " he's spooney no end on this Miss Lydon, and now I've seen her I'm not much surprised at it. I wonder how they're to be brought together again, and whether, on the whole, it wouldn't be infinitely to be preferred that they shouldn't? And yes, while I am about it, I wonder whether we can get a mile out of Graybeard to-morrow morning in two-thirty?"

A little before eight the following day saw three men, swathed in furs, and two sleighs, each drawn by a single horse, assembled at the sixth milestone on the Dorchester Road. The sleighs differed much. The foremost was made in the body like what is called in England a "sulky," mounted upon high runners. In the shafts was a big, sleepy-looking gray horse, of great power and substance, apparently for the present left to his own devices. A rug had been thrown across his loins, and the reins were loosely knotted to the top of the dashboard bar. To those ignorant of the ways of trotting-horses, a more unlikely steed could not have been produced; and nothing could exceed the contemptuous glances Jim Hawksbury cast at this apparently somnolent animal. He listened with some impatience to the conference going on between the Chirper and a tall, pale, sallow, cadaverous-looking man, who had been introduced to him as Mr. Slewerton, from the Upper Province, and inwardly vowed he had been induced to quit his bed upon a very bootless business. Mr. Cherriton, it may be presumed, had something more to go upon than his companion—it may be he has had a taste of that somnolent gray's quality; but it is certain that he regards that big-boned animal with infinitely more respect than Hawksbury does.

"And what would you say was good time if we made it this morning?" inquired the Chirper.

"Wa'al, you know," replied Mr. Slewerton, with a pronounced drawl, "he's a bad horse

to try ; he's a lazy thief, and is always two
or three seconds better on the track than
he is in a trial. Then again, that's a
·heavyish cutter. Guess you may reckon
on his being five seconds better than whatever time he makes this morning."

" And that should be——?" inquired
Mr. Cherriton.

" Two-twenty," rejoined Mr. Slewerton,
grinning ; " and then we'd just clear out
the States from north to south. He'll
be between two-thirty and two-forty this
morning ; and it's just a case of how many
seconds he's under the forty as to whether
he's worth going for."

" Do you mean to tell me that big brute
can trot over twenty miles an hour?" said
Jim incredulously.

" Yes," rejoined Cherriton, laughing, " that
I can guarantee, for I have sat behind him
in a big sleigh and seen him do it ; but how
quick he really is I don't know."

" Suppose I'd better get in," said Mr.

Slewerton, languidly, "and then we'll reel this mile off, eh?"

"Just so. Get in and sit still till you get the word 'Go!'"

"Right," rejoined Mr. Slewerton, as he whipped the rug off the gray's quarters, and, stepping leisurely into his sleigh, unknotted the reins. "Give me a caution a minute before the 'Go.'"

"Yes. Now, Jim, here's the stop-watch. Step into the cariole and keep your eye on it. Press down the spring now and loose it at the word 'Go;' keep your finger on it and press it down again at the word 'Home.'"

Hawksbury stepped into the sleigh, almost touching the snow, so low are its runners, known as a cariole, pressed his finger on the spring of the somewhat large-dialed gold watch committed to his charge—a prominent feature on which was the size of the dial for reckoning the seconds—and awaited the upshot of events.

Mr. Cherriton is driving Carlotta again. " In single harness, and when I want to gallop all the way, she's about perfect," he had observed on their way hither, " and I probably shall this morning."

Quite of that opinion, Jim Hawksbury, knowing the errand they were bound upon, until he saw Graybeard, and then he could not believe in that big, plain-headed, lazy-looking horse being a trotter.

But Mr. Cherriton steps into his cariole, and, standing up in front, gathers up his reins. " All right, Jim ? "

" All right ; both eye and finger on the watch," was the reply.

" Ready, Slewerton ? " cried the Chirper.

" Ready ! " responded that worthy, as, shortening his grip of the reins, he took the gray horse by the head, placed his heels firm against the dashboard, and sat well back in his seat.

" Then go ! " cried Mr. Cherriton.

" Hi ! ho ! whoop ! g'long ! " burst from

Mr. Slewerton's throat to Hawksbury's surprise. The snow from the leading sleigh flew back in feathery flakes. The whooping and shouting in front were incessant. Carlotta, roused into a gallop, it was soon apparent was doing all she knew, and yet more than· once did Mr. Cherriton's whip fall lightly across her flanks.

"Hi! whoop! yah! g'long!" The powdery snow flies right and left; the hedges seem streaming past, as they do when we travel by an express train. Mr. Cherriton, carried completely away by excitement, is whooping and cracking his whip like a maniac. Pouf, the snow comes blinding into their faces, thrown up by the flying hoofs of that lazy gray.

"Youp, youp! ha! hi! youp! g'long!" Crack, crack! goes Mr. Cherriton's whip. "Whoop! whoop! Hurrah! Hi, hi! youp! HOME!"

"Home!" thunders Mr. Cherriton, and down goes Jim's finger on the spring.

Slewerton drops his reins, and Graybeard, who a second before was pulling at his bit as if on the verge of running away, immediately subsides into a shamble, and becomes the picture of a used-up cab-horse, dropping rapidly into a walk, and being slightly checked, stops, and shows indications of once more resuming his slumbers.

Carlotta is harder to pacify, in spite of heaving flanks, distended nostrils, and having been put to travelling a mile quicker, perhaps, than she had ever before compassed it; she has still plenty of fidget left in her, and requires all Mr. Cherriton's attention.

Slewerton descends leisurely from his " cutter," throws a rug over the gray's loins, the reins on his back, and then lounging up the cariole, inquires what they make it?

"Two minutes, thirty-six seconds," replied Hawksbury.

" 'Tain't hardly good enough," rejoined

that worthy. "I told you, Mr. Cherriton, we could allow five seconds' discount for the horse being a slug in his trial, and the 'cutter' being heavy; but that don't bring us inside two-thirty quite, and we ought to be that to make him really good enough. He's just worth entering, and when we see what's against him we shall know whether it's worth starting him."

"You don't think this trial quick enough!" exclaimed Jim, with surprise.

"No, sir. It'll be very odd if there are not two or three entered who are well inside two-thirty. Trotting, gentlemen, is a game Britishers don't understand. That horse is good enough, I guess," and here Mr. Slewerton waved his hands, in lugubrious fashion, in the direction of the gray, "to sweep the board in the old country. Take him into the States, and they'll find a pony to beat him 'most anywhere.'"

Jim Hawksbury had certainly heard and read of the trotting phenomenons in

America; but he had no idea that what would be looked upon as horses of very great speed in that line in the British Isles, were common enough from Rhode Island to Richmond. Yet it is so, and the secret is simply this : "our cousins" teach horses to trot as we teach them to go across a country. Our trotters in England are self-inspired, and owe nothing to education.

"Satisfactory morning for you, Jim, on the whole," observed Mr. Cherriton. "You've had a lesson in trotting lore. Slewerton knows a lot, and no doubt he's right, or else old Graybeard's quicker than anything I ever saw trot yet."

"Quite so. Do you mean calling again in Sherbroke Street?" rejoined Hawksbury, in absent fashion.

"God bless me!" exclaimed the Chirper, "he's wandering. I can't knock old Maschereau up at this time in the morning. If he's out of his bed he's not out of his bath, depend upon it. My unfortunate friend, you must display some method in your madness."

"Pshaw! don't be a fool," broke in Jim, brusquely. "Of course I meant, shall you call there again to-day?"

"It's possible I may, in your interests," observed Mr. Cherriton, meditatively, as he flicked Carlotta about the flanks; "but you know it requires all my cheek and friendship, young man, to commence such marked attentions as daily visits. I shall have old Maschereau kicking me all down Beevor Hill in about three weeks, for not coming forward in earnest."

"Nonsense! Remember, I must see Clarisse Lydon."

"Just so. I'm not likely to forget it; but you'll bear in mind what I told you yesterday."

"What?" inquired Hawksbury, quietly.

"That Miss Lydon is equally determined you shall not."

"And I am equally determined she shall,' returned Jim, doggedly.

"Very good. I'll assist you all I can. In the meantime, here we are. Come in; have a wash in my rooms, and then we'll go to the mess in search of breakfast."

The twain during that meal held great council about how Jim was to attain an interview with Miss Lydon, and it was at last arranged that the Chirper was to be entrusted with a note by his principal, which Mr. Cherriton should persuade Miss Maschereau to deliver to her cousin. Verily, there is much glamour in the compliant. These two young men are both tolerably practicable and imbued with the matter-of-fact realism of their generation, and yet they must needs come to such clumsy conclusion as this. You and I, reader, I fancy, would, not being blinded by romance of any sort, have dropped our letter into the Post Office and quietly awaited the result; but even the Chirper has lost his equilibrium on finding his friend so desperately in earnest. In short, between Jack's love affair and Graybeard's dubious trotting performance, Mr. Cherriton becomes much excited in his mind, and manifests such unwonted solemnity, as to raise suspicion amongst his comrades that his own heart has gone astray.

In a day or two the ambassador seizes his opportunity, and presents his despatches; but Madeline Maschereau, who has evidently been well tutored, peremptorily declines to receive them. Mr. Cherriton, however, pleads hard for his friend, and at length the young lady, who cannot help but sympathise with so good-looking a wooer, consents to present them. Very proud is the cornet of the diplomacy, and very sanguine is Jim about the opportunity for an explanation being vouchsafed to him. Alas! when the Chirper presents himself in Sherbroke Street the following day, it is only to receive his principal's note back unopened, and to be only informed by Miss Maschereau that her cousin must beg to decline any further acquaintance with Mr. Hawksbury, both for herself and her father. In vain the Chirper asked why? Madeline Maschereau retorts sharply that she does not know, that if she did she should not tell; but that she fancies Mr. Hawksbury, after the cavalier fashion in which she heard he had treated Clarisse at Quebec, could scarcely be astonished if she declined to know him now. Calling a few days later, Miss Maschereau, in the course of conversation, quietly informs the Chirper that Clarisse has left them.

"Gone back to Quebec, I suppose?" rejoined Mr. Cherriton.

"Not at all; she has gone to stay with some friends in the Upper Province. You perhaps don't know, but I would give a good deal to hear how this quarrel between Clarisse and Mr. Hawksbury originated.

That she knew him intimately in England, and that he all but cut her in Quebec, I have heard from herself. That is the extent of my knowledge on the subject."

Mr. Cherriton made no reply.

"Somebody must have slandered her to Mr. Hawksbury, I fancy," observed Miss Maschereau, meditatively. "If they meant making discord between them, they may congratulate themselves on their success."

"I've only been just introduced to Miss Lydon," said Mr. Cherriton, gravely; "but I do know Jim from his fingers to the tips of his boots; he is the last man in the world to forget an old friendship. If he treated Miss Lydon as I am afraid he did, it must have been under some great misconception."

"You are loyal to your friend," rejoined Madeline, smiling, "and I like you for that, but the thing is all in a tangle now; neither you nor I can put it straight. It is no use talking further about it."

Mr. Cherriton took the hint, and the remainder of their conversation related to matters of more personal interest.

CHAPTER XII.

BOTTLESBY is not much of a town ; indeed, if you saw it in the summer-time I am afraid you would pronounce it, perhaps, as dull a little country town as ever it had been your ill-luck to be cast adrift in. Some three or four young ladies were to be seen flitting about the place ; the Rector or the Doctor occasionally bustled by ; three or four horsey men of the ostler type chewed straws, and exchanged remarks about that chestnut's wrung shoulder and Bill Jennings' retriever pup, outside the saddler's ; and the tradesmen generally stood at their doors openmouthed, as if gaping for fresh air, flies, or customers.

Such was its aspect in the dog-days, but when the leaf was off, and "the meets" duly announced in the county papers, Bottlesby became quite a different place. The hunting-men had established a mess at each of the principal inns; carriages of all sorts bowled through the little town—wagonettes, tea-carts, dog-carts, and pony-phaetons. Scarlet coats and top-boots blossomed in all their glory about ten through the principal street, and reappeared splashed, stained, and way-worn in the afternoon, the bloom off them, like that of a beauty's or a camellia's after a ball, when the relentless daylight steps in upon the revellers. Bottlesby was always of a sporting turn, but when the hunting season began, it, metaphorically speaking, clothed itself in scarlet. She of Babylon was of never so deep-dyed a crimson. From the Rector's wife to the chambermaid at The Bell, an you donned not pink you were no man in their eyes.

That Bottlesby had a hunt-ball was a

matter of course. When you get such a nucleus as some dozen bachelors actually quartered in a town, it would augur little for the energies of the womanhood of the vicinity if they did not compass a dance. Bottlesby hunt-ball was an institution in that country, and elderly gentlemen, the unfortunate possessors of grown-up daughters, were carried miles through cross-country roads, to their infinite discomfort, to assist in this terrible festivity. Terrible of course I mean to them, for personally I will plead guilty to some weakness for the country ball even still, while in the days when George the Third was king—no, not quite that, but once upon a time, as the story-books say — I enjoyed them immensely. Have I not ridden miles to attend them, come to infinite grief in dog-carts, and once had to do coachman to an omnibus, in consequence of the exhilarated driver, confused by strong beer and a fall of snow, persistently regarding the side of the road, where the

stones were heaped for repairing the causeway, as the Queen's highway ?   I think that
was my last experience.   The severe cold
thereby contracted has made me somewhat
shy of such sylvan revelry ever since.   The
worship of " the great god Pan " is fitted
only for our juvenile days.

The Bottlesby ball was always fixed for
quite the close of the hunting season, and
usually took place in March.   Less chance,
its promoters urged, of snow or frost in that
month ; and weather, as we all know, where
people have to drive long distances, will
deter them from coming to such entertainment.   It may be cold, and it usually was,
but however things might be anent frost,
there was generally no snow to interfere
with the Bottlesby festivity, and Bottlesby
looked upon its ball as quite one of the
county festivals.   The leading inns, two in
number, do, as may be supposed, a tremendous business upon this occasion, and
belated bachelors are even caught and

plucked by ordinary publics. The ball takes place at the town-hall, but the supper is furnished alternately by The Bell or The Mitre; the hostelry that does not provide the feast generally spreading a festive-board on its own account, which, in consequence of a liberal supply of oysters, is more in vogue amidst the wilder spirits of the neighbourhood than the regular supper at the town-hall.

Tweedle dee, tweedle dee, tweedle di, di, dum, dum, go the violins, as Lady Hawksbury, Sara, and Uncle Robert enter the room; prepared each to regard the Bottlesby ball from their own point of view. To my lady it means the exercising of a certain amount of patronage and superciliousness; to Sara it means downright dancing with all her might; to the Rector much gossiping, interspersed with judicious refreshments. It bears all the special characteristics of country balls. The grandees established at one end of the room gather round the dear

duchess, or, as it is not given to every
county to be the happy possessor of such
an illustrious lady, around her equivalent
usually speaking, too assured of her position
to trouble herself about standing upon it,
after the manner of her smaller satellites,
who deem much demonstration of eye-glass
and uptilting of the nose necessary to assert
their dignity. There are the London con-
tingent of men staying at the neighbouring
country houses, who may be divided into
two classes—the small and junior lot, who
consider it their bounden duty to talk with
a drawl, whisper to their partners that "it's
wather dwoll, you know, seeing the bar-
bawians at play;" wondering whether they
introduce a May-pole, with as much more
imbecility and impertinence as may occur to
them. Then there are that other London
division, consisting of the men (older, these)
who go in for the whole fun of the thing;
who pick out the prettiest country girls and
dance and flirt with them *con amore*,

making the ladies of their own special party wild with indignation, and filling their breasts with rancorous feeling relative to the Doctor's daughter, and those Miss Cotton-cakes, nieces of the wealthy seed factor and agricultural implement maker. Pretty girls, too, undoubtedly, many of these with all their rustic freshness still upon them; not, perhaps, dressed so well as their rivals from the big houses—it were scarce likely. They were given to design their garments from *The Queen* newspaper, and verily believed, poor innocents, that the prints thereon designated the latest fashions. Small wonder that their bright eyes and cherry lips were hardly made the most of under such delusion.

Sara Hawksbury, as may be supposed, had no lack of acquaintances in the room, both county and Londoners. A vivacious young lady, who, if not quite pretty, was decidedly good-looking—who had lots to say for herself, and was an irreproachable

waltzer—it may be easily conceived Miss
Hawksbury was not likely to sit out much.
Her partner had paused, breathless, at the
far end of the room, after a somewhat
prolonged turn to the "Croat Galop," and
Sara suddenly found herself next to Alec
Donaldson. Since the famous mistake of
the Bottlesby Cross-roads Meet, they had
often come across each other. Donaldson
had called at Ringstone Abbey, and been
cordially welcomed. My lady had gushed
over him after her manner; called him her
boy's preserver, and so on, in the first
instance, though latterly things seemed to
get a little mixed in her mind, and she
rather took up the idea that Jim had
been his—Donaldson's—in some vague, in-
definite fashion. As for Sir Randolph, he
seemed as pleased to see Donaldson as he
was to see anybody; and in good sooth,
that was not saying much, for the baronet
of late had waxed exceedingly bitter to
his fellows, and could be relied on for

tolerable civility even to few beyond his own brother; his wife and daughter most assuredly not of the elect. Still, Donaldson had dined and slept two or three times at the Abbey, and had many a bed and dinner from Uncle Robert, when the hounds met the Horeby side of the county. The Rector, indeed, had taken a great fancy to him; and, thanks to the reverend Robert's introductions, the way in which he took his own part in the hunting-field, and his pleasant manner, Alec Donaldson had made his way into the county society in a way seldom achieved by a country doctor. To be a gentleman and ride straight is a great passport in a sporting neighbourhood; but when it was known that Donaldson was simply doing duty at Bottlesby for his friend Dr. Ashford, and had negotiated the taking over of a London practice for himself, the country side took up Alec Donaldson with considerably more warmth than he could have reasonably expected. The result was that he knew most of the magnates in those parts, and had ate, drank, and slept 'neath the shadow of their roof-trees.

"Is it any use asking Miss Hawksbury if she has a dance to spare?" said Alec, as he shook hands.

"Certainly, and with pleasure," laughed Sara. "I must put you a little low down, you know; your own fault, for being so late in claiming one. My hand rarely goes begging in a ball-room 'in my ain countree.'"

"Of course not, nor elsewhere. That I was only able to get here a few minutes ago must be my excuse for not having made an earlier appeal. Your uncle is here, I presume?"

"Oh yes. You'll find him killing foxes theoretically, somewhere about the tea-room, I fancy. Number twelve, remember, and *we're not to hunt.*"

"I'll not forget the hint," rejoined Alec,

laughing ; " the sport of kings interdicted. Alas, poor Jorrocks ! "

Miss Hawksbury, with a wicked little nod, once more consigned herself to her partner's guidance, and disappeared in the vortex of the ball-room.

The Rev. Robert Hawksbury was, as his niece suggested, gossiping with a lot of old acquaintances around the door of the tea-room.

" Heard from Jim lately ? " inquired a bluff country squire, who had known the family from childhood.

" Yes, last mail ; and Jim writes the most astounding accounts of the hunting in those parts. Snake fences, whatever they may be, seem to be an ordinary impediment, which you have no sooner got over than you have to get over it again. No moral or other rectitude about a snake fence, apparently. He says that the Montreal season is about over. Fancy a country in which the season is a bare two months! He winds up by a description of a hurdle-match he saw up at Toronto ; four-foot hurdles, and built up stiff as gates. 'No galloping through them, Uncle Robert,' he writes ; 'if you do hit 'em hard, up you go *sic iter ad astra*, as we used to observe at college, when we got into a big scrape.' "

Uncle Robert's auditor looks a little askance at this story of racing over stiff hurdles four feet high. He is too courteous not to assent to that anecdote ; but he remembers that he has heard much of the fertilising powers of the snow, and it may be that its effect was equally stimulating to the imagination ; anyway, they had never raced a couple of miles over gates in the Cottlestone country. Lady Hawksbury in the meantime is inquiring in most fervid fashion after the health of her friends and neighbours ; so anxious in her interrogatories on this point, and so utterly careless as to what answer she may receive as to

increase the dislike and mistrust with which
she is ordinarily regarded, in no small
degree. Neglect to ask after people's health
if you will, as a rule that will cause little
offence ; but when you do, beware of not
attending to the recapitulation of their
ailments. If you pull the string of the
shower-bath you must not complain of
wet weather ; and when you inquire after
the state of anyone's cold, pay decorous
and patient attention to the pitiable narrative of their influenza which naturally
follows. Our ailments are a source of much
interest, and supply us infinite material for
conversation after we are well past our
zenith.

"What news have you from Montreal,
Miss Hawksbury?" asked Donaldson, as he
led Sara away for the dance.

"I have not heard for some time ; but
Uncle Robert got a letter last mail ; but
beyond Jim seems to be having a deal of
fun out there in the shape of sleighing, and

some wild attempts at hunting in a country
I should suppose from climate quite im-
practicable to hunt in, he does not say
much."

"My correspondent is more communi-
cative," replied Alec.

"Yours! Why, whom do you know out
there? Ah, stop. How stupid of me.
Mr. Cherriton, of course."

"Just so; and I also had a long letter
from the Chirper last mail, and so character-
istic of the boy, too, it sent me into fits
of laughter. One paragraph ran : 'Never
think, Alec, you know anything about
trotting. Nobody does in England. You
must come out to the West and buy your
experience as I have ; if ever you meditate
doing anything in that way consult me, I
will keep you straight.' Is not that delicious,
Miss Hawksbury? as if I ever was or was
ever likely to be concerned in anything
connected with trotting. He might as well
have implored me to refrain from balloons

or diving-bells until I had heard what he had to say concerning them."

" Very like him, though," laughed Sara. " Does he say anything about Jim ? "

" Well, he does," returned Alec, slowly ; " and I own I've been rather puzzled whether to tell you or not."

" But you have made up your mind that it is best to do so ? "

" Certainly ; or I'd never have been so foolish as to say what I have. Did your brother ever talk to you about his sojourn at Burnside when he was under my care ? "

" Yes, of course he did. Ah, I know what you are going to tell me. We have never talked about it before, you and I ; but that Canadian girl, that Miss Lydon, has turned up again. You have seen her! What is she like ? No ; never mind the galop. I want to talk to you about this."

" I'm sure, Miss Hawksbury, your brother has no firmer friend than yourself. You would not repeat anything to his detriment."

Sara made a sign of dissent.

"Miss Lydon is a very pretty, lady-like girl, and there can be no doubt Jim was rather struck with her at Burnside. Do you know he saw a great deal of her in London afterwards?"

"I have heard so, indirectly," replied Sara.

"He has come across her again in Canada; and, according to the Chirper's account, is wild about her."

"And of course she's made up her mind to marry him—scheming colonial wretch."

Allowances must be made for the irritation Miss Hawksbury experienced upon hearing such shattering of her day-dream; these dreams! aye, we often look upon them as past fulfilment; but the bitterness of disappointment is none the less when the final toppling over of such *Château d'Espagne* is demonstrated to us.

"Quite the contrary," replied Donaldson. "Jim has apparently had but one chance of speaking to her, and of which he failed to avail himself. She has kept most pertinaciously out of his way, and there can be no doubt, according to what Cherriton tells me, has no intention of his ever seeing her if she can avoid it. I do not pretend, nor does the Chirper, to in the least understand the ins and outs of this flirtation of your brother's, but the cornet writes in comical distress on the subject. You will not be angry if I quote what he says?"

Miss Hawksbury shook her head, and murmured: "No; go on."

"'Jim is awful hard hit, and raving because he cannot succeed in seeing the lady of his love. I have done my best, Alec, but Miss Lydon is evidently most determined it shall not be. We had one chance when I upset our sleigh—that is, the one in which Jim and I were—to avoid upsetting the one in which the young woman was. If I had only known she was in that other! but I didn't. I'd have upset the two, and a

reconciliation must have taken place in the
general scramble; there's an end of being
cuts when you are all rolling in the snow
together. As it was, the confounded polite-
ness, that is my undoing in this world,
prevailed. I drove into the drift to let their
sleigh go by. We rolled in the snow and
they laughed at us. *They*' (this young
philosopher of the century was alluding
to the sex generally) 'don't wax com-
passionate when hysterical with laughter.
It was desperate unlucky, and somewhat
disagreeable.'"

"I shall have a Canadian sister-in-law
after all," thought Miss Hawksbury. "Difficulties in a man's way in a love-chase are
very stimulating when the man is young,
and Jim is just the sort of age and temperament to feel them so."

"Mr. Cherriton, I'm afraid, is an indiscreet, if somewhat *thorough* confidant;
equal to all sorts of improper expedients,
apparently, to further his friend's ends; a

Leporello imbued with a taste for practical joking."

"It sounds as if Jim's case was serious," rejoined Miss Hawksbury, after a silence of two or three minutes. "I'll own I'm sorry to hear it. I had hoped he would marry somebody else, somebody we are all anxious he should marry; but if Mr. Cherriton is not utterly adrift in his impressions, I am afraid there is little chance now of that. You see we know nothing about this Miss Lydon, and that the lady will be extremely unpopular with the authorities, I can emphatically vouch for. My father gets wroth about small matters now, and is likely to be very indignant concerning this. He and Jim are on by no means amicable terms, even as it is."

"I don't think you need be uneasy about things yet," replied Donaldson. "Evident, very, that there is nothing at present between your brother and the young lady. Won't you have one turn before the galop is over?"

"But there has been, and will be again," rejoined Sara, curtly, as she rose and yielded herself to Donaldson's guidance.

The young doctor danced as well as he rode, and as they walked through the room afterwards, there were lots of the *élite* of the country who stopped and greeted the pair, and more than one fair head was smilingly bent in return to Alec's salutation. He had no lack of partners, as Miss Hawksbury noticed a little later; albeit she was not destined to take stock of Alec's or anyone else's doings much longer. Sara was good to dance most balls out, providing only that the room and the music were tolerable; and Uncle Robert always had so many friends to talk over sporting and country doings with, that he rarely found the duty of chaperon hang heavy upon his hands; but with Lady Hawksbury it was very different. She looked upon it as bad style to stay late. She had, moreover, usually got not into hot, but most decidedly chilly

water before the evening waned, and though
not very sensitive to rebuff, did feel upon
the present occasion that she had been
decidedly snubbed by the Marchioness
Chartowers, the *grande dame* of the county.
Lady Bolsiver, in answer to fervid interrogatories about her neuralgia, " so trouble-
some at this time of year," had somewhat
tartly given the inquirer to understand that
three months had elapsed since Lady
Hawksbury had thought it worth while to
call and seek information concerning it.   So,
upon the whole, my lady thought it expe-
dient to retire ; and being, like her liege,
very little given to considering the feelings
of other people on such social occasions,
she quickly despatched messengers to her
daughter and brother-in-law to apprise them
of her intentions.   Sara dutifully sought
her mother's side in compliance with the
maternal fiat, and Uncle Robert announcing
speedily that the carriage was at the door,
the Bottlesby ball was over as far as the
Ringstone people were concerned.

CHAPTER XIII.

WHAT is time? A fact. Pooh! a matter of imagination. Who of us can form the faintest conception of what eternity really means? We apply the epithet to a dull dinner-party, a heavy ball, or a stupid entertainment. People talk of interminable weeks, never-ending days, while their neighbours could tell of how these days and weeks vanished like snow in a rapid thaw.

"Slow are the winter months gliding away," mused Mr. Cherriton. "Troughton's both cynical and mendacious. I never have time for all I want to do."

Jim Hawksbury, too, was fain to admit

it was wonderful how the winter slipped away.

Time ! it is a sheer matter of how time is passed ; and though for purposes of chronology it is necessary to lay down the rule that there are sixty seconds in the hour, do we not all know better ? Have we not known hours composed of two hundred, and others of twenty seconds ? That *mauvais quart d'heure* before dinner (anathemas on their heads who prolong them), and that other at our dentist's, do you mean to say they consist of only fifteen minutes ?

Yet the two friends had each their own burdens to bear throughout that winter. Mr. Cherriton's, though lighter than his comrade's, occasioned that genial cornet much unhappiness. Contrary to the experienced Slewerton's decision, he insisted upon entering and starting Graybeard for the trotting handicap. That gentleman drove, and drove scientifically ; but his first verdict was endorsed—the horse was simply

not good enough. This was a blow to
Mr. Cherriton's pocket in the first place,
which, to do him justice, he bore with
equanimity ; but in the second it was a
blow to his pride. Mr. Cherriton piqued
himself on his "knowingness." He had
induced his fellow-subalterns to back his
nomination, and brought desolation into the
mess in consequence. The Chirper was
very rueful over this *contretemps*.

As for Hawksbury, he could not forget
Clarisse. He cursed his folly scores of times,
but that naturally brought slight relief.
He knew now that he loved this girl in
real earnest. He knew also that she re-
sented his behaviour with equal earnestness ;
and who could blame her ? To treat
intimates of a few months back as almost
strangers, is a common and contemptible
trick of humanity ; but if those intimates
have a spark of pride in them, they take
care it shall not happen again. The old
story of the nobleman, whose acquaintance

being claimed in town by a gentleman, on
the score that he had known him at Bath,
retorted that "he should again be happy
to know him in Bath," is always laughed at.
Yet, what an arrant snob that nobleman
must have been! It would be trying,
certainly, to stroll down the Row with "the
Spotted Dog" in plain clothes; but having
broke bread in his wigwam you cannot well
refuse. In his war-paint the sensation
would justify the event.

The snow is fast disappearing. Sharp
reports, like the discharge of field artillery,
come booming from the river, and Montreal
knows that St. Lawrence is waking from his
winter's sleep, and snapping the shackles
of the ice-god. The waters begin to heave,
and the ice practically blows up from their
pressure and explodes with mimic thunder.
Piled in heaps, the frozen water sweeps
down the mighty stream, with which it
rapidly assimilates. Thick in the river yet
packs the ice opposite Fort Diamond; but

about Montreal it is verging on summer. Spring in Lower Canada. is a myth. You jump from winter to hot weather, from furs to linen and calico.

Now with the summer came on this occasion, not the swallow exactly, but the Fenian; and, in scriptural language, he set up his tent over and against Montreal. He was to be seen encamped in considerable force only the other side of the Niagara river; and if the authorities had been uneasy last autumn, it may be conceded they felt even less tranquil in their minds now. Sir Richard Bowood indeed was much exercised about it. True, he had assurances from the American Government that they neither participated in the movement nor had the slightest intention of permitting it; yet why did they tolerate these camps formed with avowedly hostile intentions to Canada? It was all very well for them to claim that they must deal with the business in their own fashion; "but," argued Sir

Richard and many another leading Canadian
in those times, "why didn't they deal with
it ? When did they intend grappling with
this factious scum that denominated itself
Fenian ?" Meanwhile there was nothing
left for it but to keep a shrewd eye on these
camps, and to hold the troops in readiness
to move instantly. With all those miles
of frontier to guard, it was difficult to say
where the raid might not be projected; still,
those canvas towns the other side the Niagara
river pointed rather to an inroad upon the
upper part of the Upper Province.

As the ice cleared the waters became
open, and the gorgeous Canadian summer
fructified ; the rumours of what the Fenians
meant doing also ripened. It was not bad,
picnicing under the tents, for men accustomed to very uncertain lodgings in the
slums of New York, more especially when
the Fenian organisation found rations for
men to whom "a square meal" was an
object of much solicitude. Slight wonder

that the Fenian mob mustered in strength upon the border, and drilled and drilled with all the energy of their Hibernian compatriots. A damp squib—a mere fizzle of a conspiracy to those behind the scenes—in reality. A split in their own organisation, as it turned out at last, and no sort of support from the American Government behind it. But Sir Richard knew that the Washington Cabinet was still sore with the neutrality England had observed during their terrible struggle with the South. They held England's moral support should at least have been given to the North, and it were idle to dispute that it had been in the main unmistakably bestowed upon the South. Actively we had carefully refrained from interference, but the heroic stand of the Southern States had undeniably entrapped our national sympathies. It was quite possible that the American Government might lend themselves to abetting such retaliation as this threatened invasion

of Fenianism might afford. Sir Richard
Bowood held the situation serious, and
prepared for decisive action.

Sir Richard is placed in that most
invidious of positions — he is to be a
general of demonstrations ; but " let there
be no actual burning of powder," quoth the
authorities. Given a vacillating colonial
secretary at the English end of the electric
wire, and I'd scarce wish my worst enemy
in deadlier dilemma. The days for great
victories for constitutional Governments have
disappeared with the invention of the telegraph. Such triumphs are reserved now for
despotisms. In a European war an English
general would be commanded by a nervous
diplomatist in Parliament Street, with results
that it is not pleasant to reflect upon. In
the meanwhile, Sir Richard keeps anxious
eye on those camps the other side of the
Niagara river, and has made up his mind
that violation of the frontier must be
thoroughly dealt with.

" News, Hawksbury, news; stirring news rather," said the Adjutant-General to Jim one fine morning towards the end of May. " What's Sir Richard say to it ? "

" What do you mean ? I haven't seen him this morning," replied Jim.

" We have just received intelligence of an immense Fenian gathering at Buffalo, and an intimation that the probability is they really mean business upon this occasion. The American President has issued a proclamation declaring it illegal, and General Grant has instructions to keep a strict eye upon their movements. I fancy the Government of the States intend being thoroughly loyal to us ; but they will not interfere till they can be down upon them for actual infraction of the law."

" What bosh ! " exclaimed Jim.

" No, not altogether. It's a free country ; so is England, and you may do a deal of preliminary drilling in either before Government interfere with you. Who is to say

whether you are drilling for the defence
of the authorities or their subversion ; for
amusement or filibustering purposes ?"

But the telegraph shortly brought other
and more explicit information. It seemed
that after much speechifying and fierce
denunciation of the Saxon for some two
days in Buffalo, a body of Fenians, on the
night of May 31st, had crossed the Niagara
and seized upon Fort Erie. As to what
actual strength they were in, the Government were without information ; but they
did understand the importance of Fort Erie.

"Second edition ! Fenian invasion of
Canada ! Great success ! Capture of Fort
Erie !" sounded somewhat imposing voci-
ferated in Broadway, and made the New
York world opine that there really was a
backbone to this much-talked-of conspiracy;
but the Canadian Government were of
course aware that Fort Erie was an abandoned stronghold of former times, and open
to be taken possession of by any large-

hearted conspirator, who was armed with
a spade with which to clear his path through
the thistles. Still, Sir Richard was quite
alive to the fact that Fenians, in numbers
more or less, had made their appearance on
Canadian soil; were requisitioning (military
shibboleth for felonious confiscation of
property) horses, provisions, and liquors,
most especially liquors; that they were tear-
ing up the rails, and had cut the telegraph-
wires in the direction of Chippewa. Further
came rumours of their being in great force
near St. Albans in Vermont; and they were
reported to be five thousand strong opposite
Montreal and Edwardsburg. It was something to hear that they were destitute of
artillery, and poorly equipped; but for all
that, Sir Richard knew that any success
on their part would attract scores of the
disbanded Federal soldiers to their standard.
Once let there be an established nucleus in
Canada for them to rally round, and be the
States Government loyal as they will, it is

only too probable that they will be power-less in the matter. Given thousands of disbanded soldiers one side of a frontier thousands of miles in length, and attractive service for them on the other, and what nation that ever was could put forth a prohibitive police-force equal to the occasion?

Highly impressed with the necessity of speedily dealing with this first lot of marauders, Sir Richard not only flashes his commands along the wires, but for fear of Fenian agents having perfidiously cut these, despatches his aides and assistant-aides in all directions.

Her Majesty's 16th are ordered from Hamilton; and the 47th from Toronto are required, both by telegraphic message and messenger, to concentrate at Port Colborne. Jim Hawksbury, meanwhile, has been despatched to Toronto to call out the volunteers of that city, and to desire their colonel to bring his men forward to the same rendezvous. Having delivered which

message, it was of course Jim's obvious duty
to return to his chief at Montreal. After the
manner of more than one aide-de-camp, to
whom actual service is a new experience, he
thought he might just see the overture
before he went back to his proper place.

The officer commanding the 16th Regiment having been joined by the 27th Regiment at Port Colborne, and still being able
to hear nothing of the Toronto Volunteers,
promptly came to the conclusion that it
were better he should push forward at
once with the force under his command,
and leave instructions for the volunteers
to follow him. Reports of rail-ripping,
telegraph-cutting, and general looting—
described under the more euphonious term
of requisitioning—were rife, and he easily
ascertained that the Fenians were marching
on Chippewa. Hot on their track followed
Peacock (Colonel of the 16th and commander
of the column). If he had no artillery, he
was also quite aware that they had none ;

and though in some little uncertainty about
their actual numbers, he had no reason to
believe they were more than the force under
his command was perfectly competent to
deal with. And now occurred one of those
curious incidents that so constantly take
place in great wars. Marching with a
breast-high scent on the road to Chippewa,
hearing of the insurgents at every mile-
post, listening to jeremiads concerning the
fate of Chippewa, an he got not there in
time to prevent its being sacked, fired, or
what not, Brigadier Peacock passes a by-
lane leading to the village of Ridgeway in
the first instance, and to the bank of
the river Niagara and Fort Erie in the
second. It was up this by-lane the
Fenians, after landing, had originally come
and struck into the Chippewa Road. It
was very pardonable never to suspect that
the enemy, of whose doings you were
continually hearing in your front, had
suddenly lost heart, rapidly retreated, and

turning down the very by-lane from which he had emerged, was once more on his way to the river. At all events this idea never occurred to Colonel Peacock or any of his staff. They pushed forward as fast as they could manage to do along the Chippewa Road, leaving the rabble they had been sent to disperse quietly encamping themselves down that by-lane on the ridge from which the village derives its name. There the Fenian army requisitioned itself, more especially in the matter of fluids, wont, like Sir John, to take much sack with two-penn'orth of bread, an idea somewhat prevalent amongst filibusters generally. Colonel Peacock, meanwhile, pushing rapidly forward on what he conceives to be the track of the rebels, bivouacs for the night about eight miles beyond that by-lane, on the sides of the highway to Chippewa.

The Queen's Own Volunteers from Toronto arrived in due time at Port Colborne, only

to find that the regulars had left, and, of
course, they pushed on in compliance with
their orders, in pursuit of Brigadier Peacock,
but before they reached this famous by-
lane, which plays so prominent a part in
the history of the great Fenian invasion of
Canada, they became aware that the enemy
were occupying Ridgeway, and after some
slight reflection the Colonel of the Toronto
Volunteers resolved to attack them. Jim
Hawksbury, whose clear bounden duty it
was to return promptly to Sir Richard
Bowood, at Montreal, his orders once delivered to Colonel Booker, commanding the
Toronto Volunteers, has persuaded himself,
in the way staff-officers do sometimes upon
such occasions, that it is his business to
see the junction of the volunteers with the
regulars satisfactorily effected. That he
would influence the decision of the chief
of the volunteers was scarce likely; but
hints from staff aides-de-camp have been
known to have disastrous effects before now,

and it was scarce likely that Jim Hawksbury
would not be of the kind to suggest " Going
at them "—plenty of men of the same sort,
probably, about their chief at that moment.

General O'Neil, of the Fenian army, may
or may not have been a great general. It
is difficult to develop the qualities of a
great commander when you command a
Falstaffian array. He had at present seized
Hoffman's Tavern—a position to which, if
its name carried actual meaning, he could
depend upon his followers stanchly clinging
—as the key of his position, and thrown
out his men in skirmishing order amidst
the scrub that crowned Ridgeway ridge ;
a position of some strength in many
ways, more especially as both masking his
numbers and the quality of his troops ; a
position, too, calculated to give some con-
fidence to his ragamuffin battalions, insomuch as the shooting at men who cannot
see you is immeasurably more comforting
than shooting at men who can—apt to

inspire considerable courage this, in those who may find their own bullets telling, while they preserve tolerable immunity from the retorts of their adversaries. The volunteers speedily felt this—they were shooting at mere puffs of smoke in a thicket, but the denizens of the thicket, though making peculiarly bad practice, had, at all events, their foe in the open to fire upon. The colonel of the volunteers saw a few of his corps fall, and was totally ignorant of in what strength the enemy might be; further, he had no idea of where Colonel Peacock and his column were at this moment, and remembered, perhaps somewhat late in the day, that his orders had been to place himself under that officer's command. The Toronto riflemen, in short, were undergoing that baptism of fire most trying of all to the uninitiated; when the few first victims of the war moloch plunge or stagger in their tracks, before the tumult of combat had commenced, before the madness of

battle has quickened the pulses; and that
they were a little unsteady in consequence
may be easily conceived. Jim Hawksbury,
after a manner not altogether unknown to
staff-officers, conceived it was his business
to interfere, and dashing forward, called
upon the company nearest him to charge.
The men manifested no disposition to
comply with Jim's enthusiastic but utterly
unwarranted demand; he was a volunteer
—no officer of theirs—and had virtually
nothing whatever to do with the matter
in hand. The Fenians were more re-
sponsive; they noted the rush of an officer
to the front, waving his sword in one hand
and cap in the other; they felt the crisis
of the day was at hand, and with marvellous
unanimity discharged their firearms at a man
who showed such a shocking and dangerous
tendency to come to close quarters. Jim
dropped his sword, staggered forward, and
finally fell flat on his face, with a bullet
through his ribs, another through the calf

of the leg, and a slug in his shoulder.
Better, perhaps, that he had adhered strictly
to his bounden duty, and hurried back, his
despatches once delivered, to Sir Richard
Bowood.

At last, the Chief of the volunteers,
failing utterly to discover in what force
the enemy might occupy the scrub in his
front, seeing no signs of approaching reinforcements, and conscious that some score
or more of his men had fallen in this
futile attempt to feel the foe, reluctantly
gave the order to retire. The volunteers,
carrying off both their dead and wounded,
retreated slowly and sullenly amidst the
tumultuous and triumphant yells of the
Fenians; and thus, after a sanguinary
struggle of twenty minutes ended the
memorable battle of Ridgeway. General
O'Neil, meanwhile, though flushed with a
pardonable pride in his apparent victory,
had his own anxieties. There had not been
that influx of sturdy recruits to the green

banner with its golden harp that he had anticipated; in short he had been joined by nobody. The supporting bodies that were to follow him he could hear nothing of. He was quite aware that his force, though posted in the scrub, and liberally allowanced with "Bourbon," had wavered considerably during the combat. He knew that had the volunteers made a determined rush at his position, never a man of his command had bided the result of it. He was aware, moreover, that a column of regulars was already in his vicinity, and let the strength of that column be comparatively small, yet it was tolerably sure to outnumber his ragamuffin army. Further prosecution of the great enterprise was impossible; all he could hope was to bring himself and his men safe off, and he therefore resolved to fall back once more on the Niagara.

Colonel Peacock all this time was bivouacing, as before said, some eight miles off on the Chippewa Road, and in utter ignorance of the bloody struggle going on upon the ridge in front of Hoffman's Tavern. Thanks to there being no artillery on either side, the sound of the firing did not reach the ears of the regulars, who consequently passed a tranquil night, and awoke the next morning to reconsider the problem of what could have become of these Fenian marauders of whom they were in pursuit. The scouting parties in advance reported they could get no tidings of them whatever, but ere breakfast was over the Brigadier had received intelligence, somewhat misty, it was true, but still intelligence of the battle at Hoffman's Tavern, and instantly commenced to retrace his steps. Diligent though he might be in rectifying his mistake, he could not be more diligent than General O'Neil was in endeavouring to repair his. Brigadier Peacock's consisted in having failed to come across the Fenian commander. General

O'Neil's in having ever allowed the possibility of such a meeting. The latter, however, had made good use of his start, and when the British column reached the banks of the Niagara it was only to pick up some couple of hundred stragglers, for whom Bourbon and the seductions of Hoffman's Tavern had proved too strong. General O'Neil and his rapscallions escaped, it is true, only to fall into the hands and be interned by the American authorities. Still they did escape for the most part, and bitter things were said at the time on the subject.

It was urged that to have cut this miserable rabble off, to have annihilated the half of them, and taken the remainder prisoners, was no difficult matter ; but it was perhaps wiser discretion to let them escape back to the New York slums from which they came, although the American Government had more just cause of complaint in their being allowed to return than had it been for ever freed from such unprofitable citizens.

Such, as far as I can gather it, is the history
of the famous fight of Ridgeway, Austerlitz
of the Fenian conspiracy ; being of that
pattern common to Hibernian insurrection of
late years, from Lord Edward Fitzgerald's
sad fiasco down to Smith O'Brien and the
Battle of the Cabbages. As far as this
history is concerned it was necessary to give
some description of it, because it was therein
that Jim Hawksbury, now travelling in a
country cart, bandaged, and with little life
left in him, acquired his first knowledge of
glory and the lust of battle.

CHAPTER XIV.

THE study of the Rector of Ringstone was not altogether decorated in accordance with modern ideas. There were fair-sized book-cases, certainly, in which theological works and treatises on farming stood side by side, in which Jeremy Taylor jostled "Tom Jones," and Sterne's Sermons were cheek by jowl with the immortal " Tristram Shandy," in which commentaries and calendars seemed strangely mingled; but there were more pronounced traces of " the malignant," in puritan eyes, than those furnished by the book-shelves. Against one of the walls were pinned the outlines of some

half-score or so of big pike, cut out of card-
board, with their respective weights and
days of death neatly written thereon. A
cleverly-made gun-rack, containing some
four or five double-barrels, was in one corner
of the room, balanced by a similar arrange-
ment for driving-whips, hunting-caps, &c.,
in the opposite angle. A few sporting
prints and two or three foxes' masks also
broke the monotony of the walls.

Such little furniture as there was in the
middle of the room was good and massive;
the two principal pieces being a big leather
arm-chair near the hearthrug, and a writing-
table with a multiplicity of drawers that
stood in the window.

It was curious to mark how strewn that
table was with papers, and yet more so to
observe the order that reigned amongst that
apparently hopeless chaos when you came to
investigate it. The neat and business-like
way in which letters were labelled, endorsed,
or collected together in elastic-bands, was so

evidently the habitude of a thoroughly
business man, and the Rector was eminently
that. If he more often preached the sermons of other men than his own, why, so
much the better for his congregation, for the
Rev. Robert, as he would have been one
of the first to admit, was by no means
endowed with " the gift of tongues," by
which I mean oratorical talent, be it with
his pen or in the pulpit; but he was an
active, energetic county magistrate, belong-
ing to many boards and committees, which
entailed considerable, if curt, correspondence ;
therefore his table was generally covered
with notes, notices, circulars, and applications.
As for his cure, I fancy his parishioners
would have told you not a parson in the
country knew his people so well, and that if
his admonitions were easy in the pulpit, the
harangues he at times favoured them with
by their own firesides lacked pepper by no
manner of means. .

The Rev. Robert sits in his study this

lovely June morning, twisting a bit of yellow
tissue paper on his fingers, and quietly
thinking out what he has to do, while his
horse is being got ready. It is that yellow
bit of paper, which, duly forwarded by post
from the Rectory to town, made the Rector
cut his accustomed three weeks of London
short, and return to Ringstone by the first
train. His mind is quite made up. Never
long about that, Uncle Robert; he is merely
thinking out the details of his resolve. That
yellow paper is a cable telegram from
Mr. Cherriton, and of somewhat serious
import.

"To the Rev. Robert Hawksbury, Ringstone Rectory,
Horeby, Broadshire :

"*Jim badly wounded in a brush with the
Fenians on sixth; doctors hopeful, but make
no disguise, it is serious.*

"From Richard Cherriton, —th Hussars, Montreal,
Canada East."

Robert Hawksbury is very fond of his nephew, and has determined to go out to Canada and see after him forthwith. He is going first to arrange about his duties with his bishop, and procure a delegate, then to return to town, break the matter to Sir Randolph and Lady Hawksbury, wish his own mother, the dowager, good-bye, and be off on the ensuing Saturday for Liverpool to catch the Cunard boat. It is now Wednesday, and the evening mail-train from Horeby sees Uncle Robert once more speeding to town with all his arrangements for three months' absence satisfactorily concluded. He walks down to Rutland Gate the next morning after breakfast to inform his brother and sister-in-law of Jim's misfortune and his own intentions. Wonders a little as to how Sir Randolph will take the intelligence, for though father and son had said good-bye before the latter left for the Canadas, yet their old relations had by no means been re-established, and they had parted decidedly coldly;

Sir Randolph mutely wrathful at bare idea of domestic ukase of his being disputed, and Jim sore that his father should have refused him help in so small a matter, unless under conditions which, in his son's eyes—as doubtless they would have seemed to most sensible people—were utterly unjustifiable.

Five hundred pounds is a pitiable sum enough to sell yourself in marriage for— pitiable sum enough perchance under many circumstances; but five hundred pounds when you want it, must have it, and do not know where on earth to find it, assumes colossal attributes, and the person who may and will provide us with it assumes semi-heroic proportions. It is the same with the *pièce de cent sous*, mid those whose necessities are more circumscribed.

The Rector is first of all shown into that sanctum of the Baronet's, before described, in which, fuming over the papers and answering a letter or two, he was firmly convinced he transacted a good deal of

business between breakfast-time and lunch,
a period at which he particularly ob-
jected to be disturbed; a circumstance so
thoroughly instilled into the well-drilled
butler, that he seldom permitted infringe-
ment of the same. But with the Rev.
Robert it was another thing; he was a
known power in the domestic policy, and
very reticent of the use of such. When the
Rector emphatically declared he must see Sir
Randolph, he was shown in without parley,
the butler marvelling much in his butler's
mind as to "what was hup."

"How are you, Robert?" said the Baronet
languidly, and without rising. "Nothing
important to see me about, I suppose. Still
you know Glaston says I ought to keep
myself quiet, and that I hate being bothered
before lunch."

"I'm quite aware of all that, and you
might be sure, Randolph, I shouldn't break
in upon you unless it was something important. Jim's come to grief. No, no ! not

accident of flood or field, nor yet pecuniarily;
but there has been a scrimmage with the
Fenians in Upper Canada. Jim somehow
was in it, and I yesterday received a telegram to say he had been seriously wounded."

"Seriously wounded—Jim!" ejaculated
Sir Randolph, for the first time dimly com-
prehending that, as a soldier, his son was
liable to the misadventures of the profession. "God bless me, what is to be done?
I'll send out Glaston by the next boat if he
will go, and we won't argue about the cost;
but then again, what's to become of me?
He's the only man understands my consti-
tution. What do you recommend, Robert?
Of course you telegraphed."

"What about?" rejoined the Rector
dryly.

"Everything; how should I know? It's
the proper thing to do."

Sir Randolph, between indolence and
infirm health, was about as helpless a
creature in case of real emergency as could

be well imagined; telegraphing, special trains, and hysterical shriekings and orderings stood inscribed in his mind as energetic proceedings, without much regard to the substance of such telegraphing or commanding. Ideas by no means confined to Sir Randolph Hawksbury; that noise and bustle mean energy is a belief very common amongst humanity.

"Listen, Randolph," rejoined the Rector. "It is no use telegraphing when you have nothing to telegraph about. Mr. Cherriton or Jim's chums will, there can be no doubt, keep us informed as to how he goes on. As for sending advice from London, that is absurd; it could never get out in time. There are plenty of able medical men there, no doubt; and depend upon it, Jim is in competent hands; but it would be as well the boy was looked after."

"What do you mean?" inquired the Baronet querulously. "Some of his relatives ought to slip across and see after

him, of course; but it's impossible, my dear
Robert, in my state of health! Glaston
says, 'No over-exertion; quiet, Sir Randolph, quiet; above all things quiet.'"

The Rev. Robert muttered something not
altogether complimentary to that eminent
physician. Acute ears, indeed, might have
caught the term, "Abominable humbug."
Great men are apt to be misrepresented; and
there were not wanting sceptical folks who
pronounced the eminent Dr. Glaston, M.D.,
an eminent impostor, who, having studied
his patients' weaknesses, prescribed in
accordance therewith. "Want of tone,"
"We require a little support," "We must
be careful not to over-exert ourselves," were
observations much in accord with the in-
dolent, dyspeptic class amongst whom his
practice chiefly lay; Lenten fare and considerably more exercise being in reality all
that the majority of them required.

"No, Randolph, you can't go; but I'm

strong and can. I'm off by the next
steamer. What about my lady?"

"She shall do as she likes, Bob; but
whatever she may say in the first instance,
I don't think she will accompany you in
the end."

"I suppose I had better tell her at once,
eh?"

"If you would be so good," rejoined the
Baronet, immensely relieved to find the
whole responsibilities of the situation taken
off his shoulders. He liked his son well
enough, in spite of their present difference,
but he had no great love for either his wife
or children, except insomuch as they contributed to his schemes or comforts. No
great love, indeed, for anything at present,
except it may be the acquisition of property.
Still, such capacity for affection of kith as
the selfishness nurtured of indolence and
valetudinarianism had left him, was reserved
for his younger brother.

"Very well, then, I'll say good-bye to
you for the present, and have my talk with
Caroline. Of course I shall see you again
to-morrow. I have some few arrangements
to make, as you can well imagine, but I'm
off Saturday for certain."

Uncle Robert then went out and sought
his sister-in-law's boudoir. Her ladyship
was undoubtedly much moved at hearing
of her son's mischance and the seriousness
of his case, but the trammels of long
habitude cling to us upon all occasions,
and it was little to be wondered at that she
could not resist the temptation of a theatrical
pose. She wept and used her laced handkerchief most impressively. Declared she
must fly to her boy's deathbed. In vain
did the Rector point out that serious injuries
were by no means to be read in that ill-
omened fashion. My lady vowed she should
never know peace again unless she arrived
in time to bid poor Jim good-bye. She
was certain there was no one to take care

of him, that he lacked the commonest neces-
saries, and was in the hands of most in-
competent surgeons. When, how was she
to go to him ?

"Under my charge from Euston Square,
at 7.30 A.M. on Saturday morning," replied
her brother-in-law bluntly, who knew his
sister-in-law thoroughly.

She did not know, she was not quite
sure, she could be ready, but she would do
her best. It was terribly short notice ; still,
she could only hope to arrive in time,
and therefore the sooner they set out the
better.

"And is Randolph coming too ? " asked
my lady, toying with her handkerchief, and
looking keenly at the Rector.

"No, his health does not admit of it ;
but he says you have *carte blanche* to do
as you please."

"Yes, his health is miserable. I don't
know what I ought to do—on one side
my husband, on the other my son. Was

ever woman so tortured? the one needing all my care here, the other, alas! dying in Canada."

The Rector shrugged his shoulders as he observed: "Well, Caroline, I start from Euston Square for Liverpool, as I told you, and proceed *viâ* Cunard line, to look after Jim, on Saturday. You have the whole of the next day to make up your mind and pack your trunks. I shall call in again to-morrow, and you can let me know your decision then."

"Thank you so very much; I will talk to Madeleine about it," replied her ladyship, with complete oblivion of her conflicting duties between husband and son.

The Rector took up his hat, and could not refrain from a grim chuckle as he descended the staircase, for Madeleine was my lady's French maid, and imbued with all a Frenchwoman's horror of the wild waters; and if the practicability of being ready for an Atlantic passage was to be left to her

judgment, the Rev. Robert had no doubt
as to what that judgment would be. The
next thing, he thought, was to announce
Jim's mishap and say good-bye to his
mother. He had timed his visit to Rutland
Gate so as to arrive in Park Lane about
luncheon-time. "Yes, the Dowager is in,"
was the prompt reply to his inquiry, and
the Rector was ushered straight into the
dining-room, where he found his mother
and Letty Auriole.

"Glad to see you, Robert," replied the
old lady (I beg her pardon, I mean elder
lady). "Your place, you know, is always
laid while you are in town, and though I
have no wish to be *exigeante*, you know
equally how pleased I always am to see it
filled."

Lady Hawksbury was, of course, quite
unaware of her son's hurried visit to Ringstone, and supposed he had been about
London since making his appearance in
Park Lane some three days ago.

"Thanks ; how are you, Letty ?" replied
the Rector as he shook hands; "I have come
for something to eat, to break some bad
news to you, and to say good-bye."

"Bad news !" exclaimed the Dowager.
"Is anything really serious the matter with
Randolph ? "

"No, mother.   It is Jim who is seriously
ill.   It seems there was a bit of a fight over
the water between our people and the
Fenians.   I have no knowledge of parti-
culars, only a telegram from Mr. Cherriton,
to say that Jim somehow contrived to be in
it, and is badly wounded."

·"Ah !" said the Dowager, fetching a long
breath, "he has all a Hawksbury's talent
for breaking something or other ; but what
does Randolph say ? what does Caroline
say ?   You are going out, I can see, to look
after the boy.   Who goes with you ? "

"Randolph, as you know, mother, is not
well enough."

"Fiddledee !" ejaculated Lady Hawksbury. "The journey would wake him up and do him a deal of good; and Caroline?"

"Is not sure whether her duty does not require her to look after her husband, and is further doubtful whether Madeleine could get her ready in time," rejoined the Rector, with a twinkle in his eye.

The Dowager laughed as she replied: "That French hussy hasn't, I believe, courage to go back to her own country, much less cross the Atlantic. When do you go, Robert?"

"Saturday morning—the day after to-morrow; leave Euston Square at seven and a half."

"And the boy's badly hurt?"

"The telegram says, 'seriously wounded.'"

"He'll want good nursing," remarked her ladyship meditatively; "after all bad illnesses that is the main thing. Men are no good in such cases; it wants the supervision of a woman's eye and the loving supervision of a woman. Letty, my dear, I think we must go out and nurse Jim."

"My dear mother!" exclaimed the Rector.

"You don't mean it, grandmamma!" cried Letty.

"Young people, I do mean it very much. You can be ready, Letty, I suppose! I'm sure I can, or I'll discharge every servant on the premises."

"But, mother, you are not in earnest about undertaking such a journey at your time of life, surely?"

"My time of life, indeed!" retorted the Dowager, with mock indignation; "if the family records did not unfortunately convict me of your maternity, I'd appeal to the public as to which of us was youngest."

"Are you sure it will not be too much for you, grandmamma?" exclaimed Miss Auriole.

"There's a pleasant life before you, my dear, if I don't go. You'll find what a disagreeable young woman I can be when I try. Nonsense, Robert, my mind's made up. I'm sick of London. Sir Richard Bowood will, I am sure, make it pleasant for *me* out there. We'll go to Canada, Letty, nurse Jim into convalescence; the scapegrace owes me five hundred pounds, you might recollect; and to a mercenary old money-lender like myself that is a serious consideration. We shall have great fun, see a new country, and be back here about the end of November, or a little later. If we appear at Euston Square on Saturday morning, in due time, I presume you will take care of us, Robert?"

"Of course I will, mother; but do think a little about it," replied the Rector, gravely.

"Bless the boy, we've only time to think about packing up, if we're to be of use to Jim; besides, I don't know that it is good that you should be allowed to go off to the Far West without someone to look after you. It's no use arguing, Robert; I tell you, in homely language, we are coming too, so you must make the best of it."

"I am only too glad not to have a lonely voyage ; and now I am off. I have several things to see about, and I am sure you must have. So, for the present, good-bye."

"Good-bye," said the Dowager, as she returned her son's kiss. "We shall be true to our tryst on Saturday morning, believe me, if we don't see you again. And now, Letty," she continued, as her son left the room, "the sooner we give the maids orders to tumble our things into the trunks the better. Luckily, they are used to my erratic ways, and what we wear here will do to wear there at this time of year. No necessity for special outfit, or anything of that kind. An Atlantic passage is a much simpler affair than crossing the Channel, in the days when I was young ; of course I mean in my infancy."

END OF VOL. II.

CHARLES DICKENS AND EVANS, CRYSTAL PALACE PRESS.